Dear

Welc

Though I know an actual Buckhorn exists, mine is an entirely fictional town in beautiful Kentucky. My first Buckhorn story was published back in 2000 and the series has become a true reader favorite. For me it seemed a natural fit to combine my need to help stray cats and dogs by continuing the series with a new generation of the leading family in Buckhorn.

Through a special contract with my publisher, the advance and all royalties on *A Buckhorn Summer* will go directly to the Animal Adoption Foundation, a local no-kill animal shelter that does an amazing job healing, protecting, and loving cats and dogs until a "forever home" can be found for them.

I hope you enjoy the story, and I especially hope you enjoy knowing that by purchasing this story, you've helped a dog or cat in need. And don't miss *Back to Buckhorn*, my 2014 benefit novella, included as a bonus in this collection!

To see other "benefit books," visit lorifoster.com/benefit-books/

And to see other books in the Buckhorn series, visit lorifoster.com/connected-books/#buckhorn

From the bottom of my heart, thank you!

Lori Foster

Also available from Lori Foster and HQN Books

The Ultimate series

"Hard Knocks" (ebook novella)
No Limits
Holding Strong

Love Undercover

Run the Risk
Bare It All
Getting Rowdy
Dash of Peril

Men Who Walk the Edge of Honor

"Ready, Set, Jett" (in *The Guy Next Door* anthology)
When You Dare
Trace of Fever
Savor the Danger
A Perfect Storm
"What Chris Wants" (ebook novella)

Other must-reads

Heartbreakers
All For You
Charade
Up in Flames
Turn Up the Heat
Hot in Here
Love Bites
All Riled Up
The Buckhorn Legacy
Forever Buckhorn
Buckhorn Beginnings
Bewitched
Unbelievable
Tempted
Bodyguard
Caught!
Fallen Angels
Enticing

And don't miss a brand-new Ultimate novel from Lori, also coming soon

Tough Love

CONTENTS

A BUCKHORN SUMMER

To the Animal Adoption Foundation,
www.AAFPets.org.

Thank you for all you do
to help dogs and cats in need.
I know my contributions
are always put to very good use.
It's been a true pleasure watching the AAF grow!

CHAPTER ONE

ONE MONTH AGO today, she'd awakened disoriented in a posh hotel in Chicago. Exhausted. Tired of travel.

Lonely.

For the longest time she'd stared at the ceiling, getting her bearings and knowing she needed a break. Her stomach had burned from too much stress. Her neck hurt from the small, flat pillow.

Lisa Sommerville had known instinctively that she needed a change, so she'd gotten up, dressed, gone down to the bar and…

"Lighten up," her cousin Shohn said from behind her as he turned the small outboard motor on the fishing boat, steering around a sunken log and aiming toward the marina where they'd gas up and grab bait. "You'll have fun. Guaranteed."

On the seat in front of her, the bright morning sunlight making a halo of his fair hair, her brother, Adam, grinned. "No thinking about work, remember? If we catch you drifting off, Dad gave us permission to drop you in the lake."

Lisa looked over the side of the boat. The water was green and cool and this early in the day, fairly smooth. "I wasn't."

"Fibber," Adam said.

"That's all you think about," Shohn agreed. "But not today."

She didn't bother to correct them, to explain that her thoughts had been on her very out-of-character behavior from a month ago. On the sizzling night she'd had. On the fantasy that had come to life and still, every other minute, replayed in her mind.

"Lisa," Adam warned, again mistaking her quiet.

She looked up at the blinding sunrise splashing colors across a cloudless sky. "I'll probably take a dip on my own later." She slanted a look at her brother. "On my own, without your help, after I've put on my suit."

"You could swim in that," Shohn said, indicating her outfit of shorts and a blue T-shirt.

She turned her narrowed gaze on him, prompting him to grin like the sinner she knew him to be. They all three had dark eyes, but the similarities ended there. She was medium height, with medium-length honey-blond hair and a medium figure. Shohn and Adam both topped six feet. Adam's hair was far fairer than hers, and Shohn's was inky black.

Both men lived and worked in Buckhorn, Shohn as a park ranger, Adam as a gym teacher.

She loved Buckhorn as well, but until that fateful night in Chicago, she'd also loved traveling the country, working 24-7, earning her barracuda rep in the business world.

Icy water hit her legs, making her gasp.

"Concentrate," Shohn said, flicking his now wet fingers at her face, "or I'll grab a bucketful of water instead of just a handful."

"I was concentrating!" She brushed water droplets off her heated thighs.

"On *fun*," Adam stressed. "Not work."

Because they'd just reached the dock, Lisa didn't reply. Without waiting for the boat to steady, she stood and leaped out, a rope in hand, and secured the front of the small boat to a cleat.

Shohn did the same to the back. Adam, holding their bait bucket, hauled himself out behind her.

Every woman around stared. Always. Her cousin and brother had that effect wherever they went. Between them, she felt insubstantial, inadequate, even bland.

Which in part explained why she'd glommed onto business. In a family full of prime physical specimens, male and female alike, she was just so-so.

Except for when it came to brains and drive. Then she excelled.

Or used to. Now she considered changing it all. She could join her family in the slower, easier life of Buckhorn County, Kentucky. Doing what, she didn't yet know.

Fishing today. But tomorrow? She was not an idle person.

"We lost her again."

Sure, she needed to slow down. Her health and her very recent aberrant behavior proved she needed that change. No one in her family yet knew of her tension, her migraines, her sleepless nights.

Only that one man, a man she'd never see again—

She screeched when Shohn scooped her up and headed to the side of the dock. "Ohmigod, don't you dare!"

"You need to be dunked."

Knotting one hand in his dark hair, the other in his worn T-shirt, she growled, "Try it and you're going in with me. Or at least your hair is." She gave a tug to prove her point.

Wincing, laughing, Shohn said, "I'll jump us both in."

"No!" Okay, sure, her lake clothes, as she called them, wouldn't be harmed, but she'd braided her hair and didn't want it soaked. "Seriously," she said more calmly. *"No."*

Standing beside them, Adam crossed his arms over his bare chest. "Then no more brooding over business."

Lisa blew out a huff of breath. "If you must know, I wasn't."

"Bull."

"I was thinking of…a guy." *There*, she thought. *Chew on that.*

Both men laughed.

Laughed.

Was it so unheard of for her to be socially interested and interesting? Admitting the pathetic truth, she knew that yes, it was. At thirty, she'd never had a single serious romantic relationship.

She'd had some dates. She'd had some sex.

She'd had that one amazing night that would forever leave her warm and wanting…for more, more, more.

But she'd never been involved. And damn it, that hurt.

Mouth tight and brows angled down, Lisa turned her face away.

The laughter died.

Shohn slowly lowered her to her feet, obliging her to release his hair.

Without a word, Adam slung an arm around her shoulders and again got them heading along the dock to the gravel lot alongside the boat launch and then up the worn path to the small renovated structure that sold anything and everything boaters might need.

Hoping to clear the air, Lisa asked, "When did this change?" She remembered the structure being smaller, more weatherworn and utilitarian. Now it looked like a regular two-story house, complete with flowers planted around the exterior.

The double front doors, standing open, and the picnic tables placed all around the area made it clear the store remained, but otherwise it could have been any other home in Buckhorn.

"Rosemary sold the marina some years back to a married couple who did the additions. But they sold it a few weeks ago and retired to Arizona to be nearer to their grandkids. A new guy stepped right in and the place never closed, not even for a day. It was pretty seamless."

"Huh." So it had changed hands twice and she'd been unaware. Crazy how detached she'd been from her home. "I like the addition of a second level. Does the owner live here?"

"I dunno," Shohn said. "I've only met him a few times. He's friendly, but not real talkative, which I guess makes sense given he's a retired cop."

"You'll probably like him," Adam teased. "All the single ladies seem to."

Sure enough, as they stepped into the building, Lisa saw a trio of bikini-clad women huddled around the front counter and register, giggling in amped-up flirt mode.

She snorted. It was barely eight a.m., but the ladies were already on the prowl. The new guy must be interesting. Then again, Buckhorn was such a small, intimate town that anyone new got plenty of attention.

Shohn headed for the live bait selection, Adam went to fill the cooler with drinks and she moseyed down an aisle to pick up sunscreen. As a kid, she'd kept a light tan. As a woman who'd spent most of her time traveling from one business meeting to the next, her skin rarely saw prolonged exposure to the sun.

She remembered fishing trips from her youth and knew the guys would keep her out for hours, maybe right through lunch. She grabbed the sunscreen and a straw hat.

Heading for the snacks, she turned, took two steps—and gasped.

So did the man standing in front of her.

The big, sinfully gorgeous man.

The man with the amazing bod and killer smile and devour-you sex drive.

The man from a month ago.

Her...*fantasy*.

GRAY NARROWED HIS eyes, but the vision didn't change. Big brown eyes locked on his. Those sweet, lush lips parted. Color filled her cheeks.

It was her, but an all-new version of her. A softer, sexier version, though how that was possible, he didn't know, because every night for a freaking month he'd remembered her as so damned sexy, he felt obsessed.

Neither of them spoke. Hell, he didn't know what to say.

Let's go for round two didn't seem appropriate.

Shohn Hudson and Adam Sommerville, cousins he'd met before, suddenly flanked her.

Cocking a brow, expression cautious, Shohn asked, "Problem?"

Yeah, about a hundred of them. Gray didn't know her name, didn't know why she was here, didn't know if she remembered him or was horrified at seeing him again or if, God willing, she'd like to get reacquainted.

Adam slipped his arm around her and, yeah, that was another problem. *Don't let her be married.* Or even involved. In any way.

"You're new," Gray finally said, regaining his voice, rough and low as it sounded. His interest must've been obvious given how both Adam and Shohn looked at her again, almost as if they'd never seen her before.

She cleared her throat, worked up a very bright, false smile, and stepped away from the two men with her hand extended. "Hello. I'm Lisa Sommerville. Adam's sister."

Related? Now that she'd said it, he could see it. She and Adam shared similar dark eyes. And if they were siblings, that'd make Hudson her cousin. Nice. Only related, not involved. He could work with that.

Tucking a small box of candy bars under his left arm, Gray accepted her hand and held on. "Gray Neely." Her hands were as small and soft as he remembered, her skin just as warm.

Her scent every bit as stirring.

She tugged, and he had no choice but to let her go. "Actually," she said, now a little breathless, "I'm local. *You're* the new one."

An accusation? "So you live here?" That'd be too much of a coincidence—the first good luck he'd had in a year.

Her chin lifted. "Yes."

A slow smile growing, Adam looked between them. "Lisa's a shark, usually away wheeling and dealing with the big dawgs in business."

"She's settling back in for a spell, though," Shohn added.

"Maybe just the summer," she was quick to say.

Tipping his chin, Shohn asked, "You two know each other?"

Gray waited, and sure enough Lisa—pretty name—said too quickly, her voice a little high, *"No."*

Okay, he got that. Their time together wasn't really the sort you discussed with a brother or cousin.

"Not yet," Gray corrected, and watched her face go warm. He nodded at the hat she held. "Good idea. Going to be a scorcher today." And with that he continued on his way, restocking the candy bars on the shelf.

He heard whispering, curiosity from the guys, insistence from Lisa.

Damn, he really liked that name. It suited her.

Nice that he could now add it into the repeat fantasy that played in his head every other minute. That fantasy had been his recent salvation.

He'd met her on a desperate night during a time when nothing made sense and he hadn't known which way to turn. She'd been fighting her own demons and things had just…happened.

Scorching-hot things that had burned away his indecision and the pain of forced changes. For the remainder of the night they'd stayed tangled in erotic activity. He'd finally passed out, exhausted, sated, his brain blessedly clear of guilt and anger, her slim body held in his arms.

When he woke in the morning, she was gone.

But he'd tackled the day with a new outlook on life, and ended up in Buckhorn.

Now she was here, in the flesh, close at hand.

Glancing up, he saw the guys were teasing her and felt safe approaching again. "So how many of you are there in the area? Your family is large, right?"

Lisa moved on, pretending to consider the healthy snacks, but Adam and Shohn remained. "There's a bunch of us," Adam said, launching into a recitation of the many relatives, some of whom Gray had met, some he hadn't.

They were an impressive lot, and from what he could tell, they influenced a lot of the town. "I need to take notes to keep you all straight."

"Amber could help you with that. She's Garrett's sister."

"Met her," Gray said. Amber Hudson was beautiful, with dark hair and bright blue eyes and a smile that'd win over the darkest heart.

She also scared the pants off him. She had a bold manner and a controlling streak that kept him two cautious steps away. Not that two steps had been far enough. Within five minutes of meeting him she'd managed to get more info out of him than the rest of her relatives combined.

When Lisa looked up at him, he *felt* it. Her brows were slightly pinched, her expression uneasy. Because he'd met Amber?

Needing her to understand, to know his intent, he stepped away from Shohn and Adam and approached her. "If you stay, what will you do?"

She breathed a little faster. "Do?"

Yeah, he liked the way her mind worked. Suppressing a smile, he said, "Jobwise."

"Oh."

Now she just looked flustered, and that was so different from the confident woman she'd been with him before that he had to feel his way carefully. "You are staying, right? That's what your cousin said."

She snatched up a granola bar, stared at it and put it back.

Indecisive? That, too, was different, but he didn't mind. He took a step closer, near enough to inhale the scent of her sun-warmed skin and hair. God, he remembered that scent, how it had mingled with his own when he'd moved over her, both of them naked.

"I'm not… I don't know yet." She licked her bottom lip, glanced past him to her relatives, saw they were chatting up some other customers and stared up at him with those big, soulful eyes.

"Shh," he whispered. "It's okay."

She swallowed.

"Far as anyone knows, or will ever know, this is the first time we've met." By sheer force of will he kept his hands to himself when what he really wanted, what he needed, was to touch her, to pull her small, soft body in against his—again. "You have my word."

She released a tense breath. "Thank you." As her cousin and brother drew near again, she added, "I haven't left my job. I mean, I tried to. I gave my four weeks' notice, but they countered with another promotion. I declined and they requested that I take the summer to think about it. So I guess I'm on a hiatus."

That night in the dim hotel bar in Chicago, she'd been teeming with restless energy. But here, now, he could see the remnants of exhaustion. Bone deep. The type of tiredness a person learned to live with.

He understood that, since he'd felt it himself many times. "They must appreciate you."

She nodded.

"What is it you do?"

Before she could answer, Shohn bragged on her. "She's a top-notch troubleshooter."

"Meaning she goes to businesses that are in trouble," Adam explained, "and analyzes their problems, then tells them the best way to be more efficient and profitable."

"She's been all over the country," Shohn added. "And sometimes out of the country."

"Guys..." Lisa protested.

"I think she should loaf for the summer." Adam nudged her. "Regroup and just play."

"She's earned it." Shohn added, "Problem is, Lisa doesn't do well with idle time. Never has."

"She'd go screaming nuts in under a week."

Giving them both a quelling frown, Lisa said to Gray, "I'm still considering my job prospects."

Prospects that could take her right back out of Buckhorn? Not if he could help it. "Could I make a suggestion?"

The guys were interested, but Lisa just looked appalled. Mind made up, he forged on. "I haven't been here that long and I'm still learning the ropes. If you're related to those two, then I assume you know everyone in town, and most of what there is to know about catering to vacationers."

She opened her mouth, but it was Shohn who said, "She does."

Adam added, "She's driven her fair share of boats, launched them, too, and even worked on them a few times with our uncle Gabe."

"Gabe, the handyman." Gray had met his daughters, all three of them. They were very pretty girls who flirted playfully. And they were all too young for him—not that he'd been interested anyway.

"When my uncle Jordan married Lisa's mom, she was still a kid," Shohn explained. "So she grew up around here. She knows everyone."

"Jordan, the vet?"

"Yup," Shohn said. "He has a real nice way with animals."

So one of the icons was her dad? "Got it."

"And," Adam continued, "being the overachiever she's always been, she's organized plenty of community activities with our uncle Morgan, back when he was sheriff and since he's been mayor."

Morgan, the big, badass protector. *Who the hell wasn't her relative?* Gray said only, "Met him, liked him."

Shohn said, "She's also—"

"Stop selling me!"

Her brother and cousin gaped at her. Grinning, Gray shook his head. "Amazing to me that either of you have hooked up. Not smooth, guys. Not smooth at all."

Adam scowled. "Now wait a minute. I wasn't—"

"It's okay," Gray assured him. Hell, he was already sold. It didn't require a pitch. Then to Lisa, he asked, "Why don't you come by tomorrow morning, say around six before I open, and we can discuss it?"

Her eyes widened. Both men stayed mute.

"The pay won't be what you're used to, but the work

won't be, either. You want to enjoy the summer but also stay busy, right? I figure we can probably work out something fair. I'll be flexible on what hours you need to be here."

Amazingly, her eyes widened even more.

Cute as well as sexy. He could get lost in those dark eyes. In her slim throat, a pulse thrummed wildly. Her gaze remained fixed on his, and hell if he'd look away first. Didn't matter to him if they stood there all day.

Shohn nudged her, maybe a little harder than he meant to given that she stumbled.

Startled, she turned and smacked him. "What is *wrong* with you?"

"Me?" Shohn pointed at her. "You were the one gawking."

She flared. "I was not!"

Rolling his eyes, Adam said, "Yeah, you were."

Gray grinned. "You're all close, huh?"

"Very," Adam said with what sounded like a belated warning.

Having been a cop in a shit area rife with violent crime, Gray didn't pay a lot of attention to bluster. "What do you say, Lisa?" As an incentive, he added, "I promise to keep you busy without overworking you, and if you enjoy the lake, well, then, it could feel as much like an extended vacation as not."

Put on the spot, she finally nodded. "All right. Fine. I'll be here at six and we can discuss it."

"Not too early for you?"

Adam snorted. "She'll just be finishing up her jog."

Huh. So she liked to run? They had that in common. Gray wanted to know every little thing about her, but he could be patient. Maybe.

"If you're ready, I can ring you up."

Everyone followed him to the counter, and a minute after that he watched her go—his gaze glued to her small rounded butt in the short shorts. Damn. He remembered that sweet behind all too well, how it had fit in his hands, the tantalizing contrast of soft and firm.

With any luck at all, he'd be getting familiar again real soon.

CHAPTER TWO

LUCKILY NO ONE was around when she untied the small fishing boat and pushed away from the dock. It took three pulls on the cord before she got the motor going, then she settled onto the hard wooden seat and started down the lake.

She could have used any of the boats; the family collectively had three inboard boats, two pontoons and a variety of rowboats and fishing boats. But this particular one was the quietest and she'd as soon not draw attention. She'd done enough of that already.

The sun had just started to rise from behind the hills, sending fingers of crimson and gold to cut through the lavender dawn and play across the calm surface of the lake. Taking it slow, Lisa watched a fish jump, saw a few birds diving, turned her face up to the warm, humid breeze.

She'd always loved the fast pace of her high-pressure job.

But she also loved the peace of the lake, and maybe it was past time to find a better balance between the two.

After showering off the sweat from her jog, she'd put on sunscreen and a touch of makeup. It hadn't been easy, dodging all the curious questions and over-the-top speculation from Adam and Shohn yesterday. They'd teased, harangued and outrageously guessed without ever once coming close to the truth.

That she'd had a sizzling-hot one-night stand with a total stranger who had now, by the fickle hand of fate, relocated to her hometown.

Shohn and Adam were both utter hedonists, open in their own sexual pursuits. But when it came to her—or any of the women in the family, really—they played deaf, dumb and blind, at least with matters of sexuality. If she told them the truth, they'd be stunned, but she knew with complete confidence that they wouldn't judge her harshly, would in fact back her up in anything she decided.

She loved them, but that hadn't made it easy fending off their nonsense, all while lost in the reality of the situation.

It felt good to be home.

It felt…something altogether different knowing she'd shortly see her fantasy man again.

He was here, in Buckhorn, where she considered starting over.

He hadn't forgotten her.

He wanted her to work with him day in and day out.

Did that mean he hoped to pick up where they'd left off, as if she'd be that easy?

Or did it mean he wasn't interested and spending that much time with her in close proximity wouldn't make him as lust-crazed as it would her?

No, she couldn't believe that. Even Shohn and Adam had noticed his interest. And commented on it. Repeatedly.

"Lisa has an admirer," Shohn had said in a childish singsong voice.

"All the single ladies will be so sad to know he's already hooked," Adam had added while patting a hand over his heart. "Guess I'll just have to console them."

"I think it was love at first sight."

"Wait until he finds out she's smarter than him."

"And more motivated."

"And better paid."

Finally Lisa had willingly gone over the side of the boat, opposite from where they'd cast their fishing lines. Ignoring their calls, she'd swum to shore and pretended to consider walking back until they both begged her not to. If it hadn't been for the cow patties everywhere she tried to step, and the occasional spider web stretched between colorful weeds, she would have walked. But she wasn't an idiot.

Just embarrassed. And overcome with lust. And now even more fixated on her fantasy man.

Gray Neely.

On top of being the sexiest, most gorgeous man she'd ever met, he was also kind and considerate.

He'd willingly let her off the hook, promising not to speak of their previous acquaintance.

He was also macho, a man's man, easily meshing with her brother and cousin. How he'd looked…

She drew in a shuddering breath, filling her lungs with country air, and again pictured him in her mind. Rugged beard stubble. Alert gray eyes, focused on her. Hair longer and more disheveled. Loose board shorts and laceless sneakers, his shirt open, his muscled, hairy chest bare.

Damn, but her mouth watered, and she was so distracted she didn't dock as smoothly as usual. A frog leaped away as she drew a line through the cleat on the dock and secured the boat. A few more deep breaths and, hiking her canvas tote bag over her shoulder, she climbed out of the boat.

From the shadows of the gas pumps three docks down, a deep voice said, "I figured you'd come by water." Shirtless, barefoot, wearing only trunks, he pushed to his feet and strode toward her. His dark hair was wet, slicked back, his sinner's eyelashes spiked, his beard even more noticeable.

He stopped only a few feet from her, his gaze taking a lazy stroll from her braided hair down her body to the flip-flops on her feet. "Whenever I thought of you—and I did, often—I saw you in a business suit, your hair contained, your look professional. I liked that look a lot, especially since it was so different from the woman you became in my room."

A wild woman, that's what he meant, because that's what she'd been. Her breath stalled. "Voices carry," she whispered. "We can't talk here on the lake."

He held out a hand and, feeling as risqué as she had that night a month ago, she took it. God, she remembered his hands, so big and strong, a little rough from work, but warm and gentle as they'd touched her. Everywhere.

Silently he led her up to the store, and with each step she took, her heart jumped harder, faster. Low in her stomach, butterflies battled.

She was thirty years old, but she'd never, not once, experienced desire like this. Only with him.

One of the double doors stood open and as they stepped inside, Gray closed and locked it. Her breath caught and anticipation sharpened.

No lights were on and without the sun coming through the windows, it remained dark…and intimate.

He slowly backed her up to the wall and cupped one hand to the side of her face. "As I was saying."

Lisa felt his breath, the warmth of his big body, and had no idea what he was talking about.

"I like seeing you in these short shorts, and I like your hair like this. You were sexy before, but now you're earthy, too, and I want another taste."

After saying all that, he waited, giving her time.

Lisa nervously, anxiously licked her bottom lip—and saw his gaze sharpen.

"I remember you with short hair," she whispered. "Clean-shaven, polished." She reached up, smoothing back a lock of wet hair that had fallen over his brow. "Now your hair is shaggy, you're already tanned, and this beard scruff…" She coasted her thumb over his bristly jaw, feeling the tease of that rasp deep inside herself. "Not only are you not in a dress shirt, you're shirtless, and honestly, it's making me a little nuts."

"Nuts is good." He moved closer still but didn't quite touch her. "I was waiting on you, remembering how it had been, thinking of how it could be again, and got myself so worked up that I had to jump in the lake to cool down."

Lisa smiled. Little by little, the same chemistry she'd felt that night in the bar came sneaking over her. "I was stunned to see you here."

He nodded. "Stunned, but pleased." Both hands now cupped her face and he murmured huskily, "I've missed you."

It saddened her to say it, but they both needed a reminder of the truth. "You don't even know me."

"Not true." Gray slowly lowered his head until his nose touched her temple. "I know your scent, the feel of your skin, and how you taste."

His lips lightly grazed her cheek, making her shiver.

Near her ear, he whispered, "I know the sounds you make when you come."

She released a shuddering, broken breath.

"Yeah," he said with satisfaction. "That's how it starts." He trailed his fingertips down her shoulder to her elbow, then under her breast and over her frantically pounding heartbeat. "It ends with sweet, rough, broken moans and you holding me tight until the pleasure is over."

The way he said it, she *felt* it. "Yes."

"I want it all. Again."

As his hand covered her breast, his palm teasing her nipple, she nodded and admitted the truth. "Me, too."

"WE HAVE AN HOUR." It wasn't long enough, but it was better than nothing. He needed her. Bad.

Right now.

But she didn't move. In fact, she seemed to be holding her breath.

When he looked down at her, Gray saw her eyes closed, her bottom lip caught in her teeth, her expression sweetly agonized.

He continued to cuddle her breast while raining small, damp kisses down her jaw and her throat to her shoulder. Jesus, she smelled good, like the fresh outdoors and musk and every fucking fantasy he'd ever had, all rolled into one.

But damn it, she still didn't say anything, and as bad as he wanted her, he wanted her to feel the same.

Time to rein it in. Wasn't easy, but he asked, "You need some time?"

She nodded, then shook her head, then groaned. "I don't know."

Well, that was answer enough. "It's okay. I can wait." It'd kill him. A dozen times over. But if that's what she needed—

"That night..." Her eyes opened, full of pleading confusion. "That wasn't me."

"It wasn't me, either." He dropped both hands to her waist—safer territory—and put his forehead to hers. "It was just...right. The right time, the right person." He had to kiss her, just once, so he did. Not too deep, but far from a peck. And far from satisfying. "The right thing to do—for both of us."

"I've never done anything like it before."

For a novice, she'd been damn good. Great. Mind-blowing, in fact. "I don't exactly make a habit of it, either." He smiled, realizing something. "I like your name."

Her laugh was muffled against his throat. "I like yours, too."

"I meant what I said." With two fingers under her chin, he brought her face up. "It's nobody's business but ours."

She nodded. "This is my home, Gray. My entire family is here."

"I know. Everywhere I go, I trip over one of them." He kissed her again, all the while telling himself he had to stop that. Except that she kissed him back and damn, that nearly killed his resolve not to push her. He eased back, a little more breathless. Harder. "I like them."

Dazed, her gaze on his mouth, she asked, "Who?"

So cute. So fucking hot. Eventually she'd be his again. He had to believe that. "Your family."

"Oh. Right. Yeah, they're all terrific." Rubbing at her forehead, she admitted, "None of them would ever expect this of me. I've been so singularly focused on my career, I never made much time for relationships."

He paused—and she shot her gaze to his.

"Not that this is a relationship. God, no. I mean..."

He loved how she blushed.

A little desperately, she said, "It was just sex."

"That felt like more?"

Time stretched out with neither of them confirming or denying that.

Until finally, an eternity later, she nodded. "Yes. It felt like more."

Her hand opened on his chest, the touch now familiar, bringing all those other touches to the forefront of his mind. She'd been bold, curious, and she'd burned him up.

He covered her hand with his own. "To me, too." So many times he'd regretted not getting her name or contact info. At the time, both of them had enjoyed the anonymity and the relief of distraction.

He'd realized too late that he wanted more, because she'd already gone. Now that he knew her better and understood what an anomaly it was for her to indulge in a one-night stand, he understood why she hadn't stuck around.

"Will it freak you out to know I thought about you a lot?" Her thick lashes swept down, hiding her eyes, and her voice was barely a whisper. "Every night, but sometimes during the day, too."

He wasn't freaked out at all. Just the opposite. "Glad

to know I wasn't alone in that." Another kiss, this one longer, deeper. *Hot.* He licked his tongue along her bottom lip, then just inside. Her lips parted more, and he sank in, hungry, needing this. Needing her.

She moaned.

"It's okay," he told her as he readjusted, aligning his body to hers, drawing her closer. "It's just a kiss."

"Just a kiss." Her arms came around his neck and, helping with the embrace, she went on tiptoe.

Time slipped away. If he wanted her to work with him—and hell, yeah, he did—he needed to iron out a few details before customers started showing up.

Again cupping her face, he ended the kiss by small degrees, then drew her head to his chest. He gave himself a few seconds to catch his breath and clear the fog of lust before he said, "If I could make another suggestion?"

"Another?"

He liked her braid. It was a little loose, a little sloppy. He ran his hand along the length and enjoyed the silkiness of her hair. "The first being that you work with me."

"Oh, yeah. That."

"Yes, that." He took a step back to see her but kept a hand flattened to the wall beside her head. "And if you agree, then how about we start over?"

She shook her head. "With what?"

"Yesterday is the first day we formally met." And now he had an opportunity to know her, really know her.

Along with her million family members.

Fighting off a laugh ripe with embarrassment, Lisa

covered her mouth and whispered, "We did that without even knowing each other's names."

Liking her laugh—liking *her*—he said, "I know."

She snickered. "'Course you do. You were there."

"There, and very actively participating." Backing up so that he wouldn't pressure her again, Gray leaned a hip on the ice cream case and smiled at her. "I didn't need your name. But everything else..." His smile faded. "I needed the rest of it in a bad way. So thank you. You don't know it, but you turned me around."

Inching closer, she asked, "What does that mean?"

Hard to explain, especially since he didn't entirely understand it, but he gave it a shot. "I was..." He wouldn't say lost. That sounded real pansy-ass. "...at loose ends." *And struggling to get my head on straight.* But again, that made him sound far too weak. "I needed a change, but I'd been resisting and fucking brooding about it and if you hadn't showed up I probably would have gotten shitfaced and then gotten up the next day and carried on as usual. But after you..."

Those big, dark eyes watched him with gentle curiosity. "After me?"

"Everything felt different. Me, my situation."

"What situation is that?"

He shook his head. No way would he lay the heavy stuff on her. Not now, maybe not ever. "I was ready for a change of pace, and so here I am. But I had no idea I'd find you here, too."

She tipped her head and that silky braid fell over her shoulder, the tip resting against her breast. "Shohn and Adam said you were a cop?"

"Yeah." He'd thought to retire from the force when

he hit his midsixties. Not with an injury. Not with rage consuming him. Not with his best friend gone forever.

Now very near, Lisa asked, "Not anymore?"

He shook his head again, but that didn't suffice, so he said, "No."

Her eyes went softer, darker. She touched his arm. "You're from Chicago?"

"No, but my partner was." He pushed off the case, moving away from her and the comfort he didn't deserve, giving her his back. "I'm originally from Cincinnati. I was only in Chicago for his funeral."

He didn't hear Lisa move, but he felt the light touch of her small hand on his back. "I'm sorry."

Done with that subject, Gray turned to face her and gestured at the shop. "The hours are flexible. Minimum wage to start, but I'm open to promoting you if things work out."

Her lips twitched. "Wow, such a…great offer."

"You'll be working with me most of the time."

"There is that."

She considered it a perk? Because he sure as hell did.

As if thinking it out, she began to pace. "Like you said, my family is everywhere, and never, not in a million years, would they ever think I'd do…what we did."

"That just means I know you better than most." He'd already told her it was their secret; she'd either trust him on that or not.

"In some ways, you do. But for the most part, we're still strangers."

Didn't feel that way to him. "We could do a trial run. Take a week or two just to get to know each other." He didn't need that, but it looked as though she did. Patience, he reminded himself.

Her expression perked up. "A trial run? For the job?"

"For us," he explained. "I'd be completely hands-off. That is, unless you say otherwise." Dead serious, he admitted, "The second you say you're ready, I'm full go. But until then, for all anyone will ever know, we just met."

"You'd be doing all the giving."

Heat rolled through him, making his voice gruff. "Believe me, I remember the payoff, and lady, you're well worth the wait."

Again her face warmed, but she smiled. "Gorgeous, generous and a charmer, too. How am I supposed to resist that?"

"You're not. So tell me, Lisa Sommerville. You wanna work for me?"

"You know, Gray Neely, I believe I do."

"Great." Hearing voices outside, he strode to the doors and opened them. "You can start right now."

THE MORNING WENT off without a hitch. It was, in fact, enjoyable to jump in on one of the busiest days on the lake. As a kid, Lisa had been to the shop so many times that she knew the layout, which hadn't changed much, caught on quick to restocking and enjoyed her turn at refueling the boats.

It also impressed her how Gray handled things. He was friendly with the customers, making an effort to remember names and relationships, deferential with the elders, patient with the kids and judicious with the flirting hordes of women who descended on him.

Okay, so maybe there weren't actual hordes. But there *were* a lot of them, and to her dismay, none of them appeared to need time to think about it. Most of the women were unknown to her, vacationers there for the summer or maybe just a day.

But a few others were women she'd grown up with. Even April and Kady, two of her uncle Gabe's beautiful blond bombshell daughters, came in.

It was a joke in the family, how her uncle Gabe had been such a handful and a ladies' man and now all three of his daughters were miniature, more feminine versions of him, which meant they turned heads everywhere they went.

Gray, however, treated them with the same reserved, respectful politeness he used with the rest of the women.

All except her. With her, he smiled more warmly, and more often. And she caught him constantly watching her. Each and every time their gazes met, she felt the heat and need like a growing, combustible force.

Did she dare indulge in another fling with him?

Did she have the willpower to resist?

Later that day, around suppertime, her uncle Morgan's daughter, Amber, showed up. The opposite of Kady and April, Amber had long, sleek dark hair and amazing blue eyes. Also unlike Kady and April, Amber wore a sundress instead of a bikini. She still looked like a model, and Lisa still felt drab in comparison.

Amber spoke to Gray only for a minute, then swooped in on Lisa. "You're really working here?"

On tiptoe, straightening the shelf of hats that had been displaced by customers, Lisa nodded. "I really am."

"For the whole summer?"

Knowing Amber and recognizing that tone, Lisa turned to face her cousin. "That's the plan, but Amber, seriously, do *not* start playing matchmaker."

At that, Gray looked up and, frowning, put aside some receipts and headed toward them.

"But I have the perfect guy! Actually about a dozen perfect guys."

"No."

"Don't be a stick in the mud. You always work and never have time, but if you're right here anyway, you at least have to meet them." Holding up a hand, Amber insisted, "I won't take no for an answer. A casual meet and greet, that's all. I know! I'll invite them over to the Sunday family picnic."

Nearly every Sunday her entire family gathered together. Both her uncle Sawyer and her uncle Morgan had houses near the lake. Her cousin Casey did, too, but his was smaller, not really equipped for the big crowds of her far-reaching clan.

Dreading the possibility of having some hapless guy pushed on her, Lisa turned to Gray and said, "Sorry, but I already promised Gray that I'd work on Sunday."

Amber's face fell.

Gray slid right in there. "It's true. I'm sorry. I didn't realize there was a special function." When Amber gave him a speculative look, he shrugged. "Sundays are busy for us."

"Hmm." Amber didn't look convinced. "We all get together on Sundays. That is, anyone who isn't busy. Uncle Sawyer sometimes has patients, and Dad sometimes has business out of town that won't wait. But around Buckhorn, most everyone closes down on Sundays."

"Not the vacationers."

"No, they're always around, and they never think to get what they need before Sunday." Amber looked from Gray to Lisa and back again. "How many days a week will Lisa work?"

Lisa said quickly, "I like to stay busy. You know that."

"Mmm-hmm. So…five days?" Amber's blue eyes measured them both. "Every day?"

Lisa had no idea where Amber was going with this, only that she was definitely going somewhere. How to answer? Very unsure, she said, "Um…yes?"

"Every day. Wow. You really are a workhorse." Turning to Gray, she added silkily, "Lucky you."

Gray frowned. "When she needs time off, I'll do my best to accommodate her."

"But not this Sunday," Lisa rushed to clarify.

"No worries." Looking smug, Amber gave her a hug, turned to pat Gray on the shoulder and on her way out, said, "I'll see you around."

As soon as her cousin cleared the doorway, Lisa dropped back against the shelves with a groan.

"Trouble?" Gray asked.

"If you knew Amber, you wouldn't have to ask."

"Don't worry about it." Gray, innocent and unaware, said, "What can she possibly do?"

CHAPTER THREE

EVERY. SINGLE. DAY. For a week. An entire week!

That's how long Gray had to suffer through seeing each eligible guy in Buckhorn County paraded through his store for Lisa's approval.

Amber changed it up to keep them guessing, one day coming first thing, then during lunch, once toward suppertime, and so on. Lisa couldn't plan ahead to avoid her, because she never knew when Amber might show up with the hopeful swain in tow.

Each time Lisa was unfailingly polite to the guy without offering encouragement, while also giving her cousin death stares. The guys weren't deterred. Not that Gray blamed them.

Lisa was a catch. Although the better he got to know her, the more he realized that she didn't know it.

The week that Gray had hoped to use to win her over had instead been consumed with Amber's antics.

On the Monday of the following week, Gray waited for Lisa outside, determined to catch her before she reached the front door and dug into her duties. It was easy to see how she'd advanced in the business world. She wasn't afraid of hard work, seemed tireless and got things done with little fuss and efficient grace.

He liked it that each day she came to work by boat, even once when it rained. Yes, she was a polished, sophisticated and accomplished businesswoman. But she was also nature's child, earthy and real, not afraid of getting soaked by a summer storm.

When necessary, she waded thigh-deep into lake weeds, getting mud between her toes. She helped a kid unhook a fish, showed another how to bait his hook, explained the proper attachment of a ski line to a family of five and launched a boat for a vacationer who'd never done it before. Gray had stared in mixed awe and pride as she'd backed the car and trailer down the ramp, put the car in Park and then gone around and released the brand-new boat, using a lead line to position it alongside the dock, then tied it off.

While the owner of the boat, his wife and three kids stood there watching, Lisa pulled the car out and parked it in the lot, returned the man's keys and waved off his gratitude.

Astounding. And sexy. A take-charge woman got him every time.

Granted, he'd rather she put all that energy and focus to work in the bedroom, or on the kitchen table—hell, the dock at night, with the stars overhead, would suit him just fine.

The better he knew her, the more he liked her. The more he liked her, the more he wanted her.

In so many ways, she surprised him. Good surprises.

In a short time he'd learned that Lisa wasn't afraid of fish, worms, snakes, turtles or any of the things he was used to women screeching over. However, she kept a respectful distance from spiders. The one time she'd requested he deal with an insect, she hadn't wanted it killed, just relocated outside.

He loved how she laughed, how she analyzed a shelf before filling it to best utilize the space and how she dusted her hands off on her very perfect rear end.

He even liked how she looked when perturbed, as she sometimes was when she felt people weren't making safe choices.

This week, he decided, would be different. He'd manage more than small talk. At the very least, he'd steal another kiss. Or two. And if that worked out, well, who knew?

So that Monday morning, Gray waited on the end of the dock, his bare feet dangling in the tepid water. Anticipation thrummed through his bloodstream as he listened to the familiar purr of a motor drawing near.

Lisa was early.

Standing, he stared ahead, sexual tension ramping up, and then he saw the small boat cutting through the glassy surface of the lake. It caused a rippling wake that stirred the reflection of the bright lemon sunrise behind her. Her honey-blond hair glowed with the light of dawn and she looked so sweet, so damned serene.

Damn, he needed to have her again. Soon.

She lifted a hand when she saw him, her lush mouth curling into a smile. While a giant heron soared overhead and carp lazily crested the water, she parked the boat and tossed him a line. He secured the front and she tied off the back.

Small docks lined the entire shoreline of the marina's property to accommodate boaters coming in for supplies or gas, or for those who hung out to fish. Lisa had made a habit of parking at the one farthest away. That left them beneath several towering elms that offered shade to midday fishermen.

He extended a hand and Lisa took it, allowing him to help her out of the boat and onto the dock.

Today, with her usual shorts and flip-flop sandals, she wore a peach-colored camisole top that laced up the front and sported a loosely tied bow at the top. The outfit was innocently provocative and made him burn.

Keeping her hand in his, he looked her over with appreciation. "You left your hair loose."

With her free hand, she touched it, smoothing one side behind her ear. "I envy Amber and Gabe's daughters. They all have such gorgeous hair."

Hotter by the second, he said, "As do you."

A crooked smile showed her uncertainty. "There's no comparison and you know it. Amber's hair is dark enough that it has blue highlights in the sun. Kady, April and Brianna are the opposite, blondes so pale it's hard to believe the color is real. But me, I'm just…wishy-washy dark blonde. And no, I'm not fishing for a compliment, just stating the obvious."

"Then I'll state the obvious, too." He brushed his thumb over her knuckles. "There's not a single thing wishy-washy about you. I love your hair. How it looks and how it feels." He kept remembering the feel of it in his hands as he rode her slow and deep, and each time he got semihard. But he kept that part to himself. "Your hair inspires fantasies."

Her laugh told him she didn't believe him. "Thank you. It's not that I'm insecure."

About most things, he'd agree. But there was something, some hidden uncertainty, when she talked about her family. "No?"

She shook her head. "It's just that the clan is made up of some really great genes. But that wouldn't affect me."

Not understanding, Gray decided it'd be best discussed with more privacy. "Come here." He led her to a bench halfway up the hill, away from the water that echoed every word. Tugging her down beside him, he asked, "Okay, why wouldn't it affect you?"

"My family?" She smiled again. "You fit in so perfectly, I forget you're not from around here and don't know. See, Dad married Mom when I was six. I'm family, 100 percent, but I'm not blood related."

He recalled Shohn mentioning it, that her mother had married when she was still young, so she'd grown up in the area. "So Jordan is your stepfather?"

"Technically. But Adam and I don't think of him that way. He's just… Dad."

"I'm glad." Unable to stop himself, Gray stared at her mouth. "So he's happy to have you home?"

"Everyone is." She wrinkled her nose. "I'm the oddity, you know. Once, ages ago, my cousin Casey lived away from Buckhorn for a while. But it didn't last. The rest have always been more than content to settle here. They're all supportive, but they've never understood why I ventured away."

"Do you know why?"

Troubled, she shrugged, looked away. "Not really."

Gray teased a kiss over her temple and that brought her attention back to him. He smiled. "You liked your job?"

"I loved my job." She sighed. "Right up until I didn't."

"What changed?"

"I don't really know. Instead of feeling pumped about some of the challenges, I got fatigued. Things would happen and instead of being motivated, I'd get annoyed." She shook her head. "I started getting sick, too."

"Sick how?"

"Bad headaches, nausea." She flattened her mouth. "High blood pressure, too."

Shit.

"And I could never seem to sleep. How dumb is that? Me, the one who thrived on pressure, getting stressed out." Making a face, she whispered, "It made me feel weak."

"Only because you're so strong."

She laughed. "I didn't feel strong. I felt pathetic. Like a stranger in my own skin. Does that make sense?"

"Yeah, it does." Because that's how he'd felt, too—until he met her. He lifted her hand, kissed her palm. "You're okay now?"

"Yes." She drew a bolstering breath. "Ever since that night with you, the night I decided I needed a big change, I've been more relaxed, sleeping better. Well, mostly sleeping better. But sometimes..."

"Sometimes what?"

"Sometimes *you*."

Gray studied her, how the morning sunlight shone on her face. "You said you still think about that night."

"Think about it, dream about it. About you." She stared at him with those dark, consuming eyes, then sighed. "A lot."

"It was memorable for me as well."

Suddenly antsy, she pushed to her feet and walked to a tree, leaning on the trunk while watching him. "We were supposed to use this time to get to know each other."

Gray stood but didn't approach her. "I did."

"How? We've been swamped."

"You think I haven't paid attention? Not for a second am I ever unaware of you."

Her gaze locked on his. "I've seen you watching me."

"I can't help myself." He didn't point out the obvious, that she knew because she'd been watching him, too. "I know you like two cups of coffee first thing in the morning."

Her mouth slipped into a smile. "True." Her gaze

flickered to his chest, then away. "I know that you only shave every third day."

"Unless there's a special occasion." Nice that she'd noticed. And given her interest in his chest, he wished he hadn't pulled on a T-shirt. "It bothers you?"

"I think it's sexy."

"Now, see? I know that you're honest, too. That you say what's on your mind."

"Actually, I didn't mean to." Again her gaze dipped to his body and she let out a breath. "Around you, I just forget myself."

He smiled. "I figured out, pretty quickly, that you know a hell of a lot more about boats than I do."

Playing along, she said, "I figured out that you're a quick learner." She didn't leave it there. Brows together, she added, "And you have a knack for just *knowing* things. Like, you look at a trolling motor and somehow figure out that the propeller got tangled in lake weeds. Or that the breaker had blown on the freezer chest—and how to fix it. Or the most expedient way to get a fishing line out of a tree."

"Those were all common sense."

"A rare commodity."

"And you?" Slowly, not wanting to push her, Gray moved closer. "Is there anything you can't do?"

Her chin lifted. "I can read instructions, so no. Unless it involves brute strength." She flexed her arm, showing a small biceps. "It's the truth, I lack muscle."

Sliding his fingers around her slender arm, he tugged her closer. "I have a feeling that, if necessary, you'd figure that out, too."

Staring up at him, she whispered, "There's usually a way."

"Would it be rushing things too much if I kissed you?"

She breathed a little faster. "I was hoping you would." And before Gray could make a move, she came against him, her arms around his neck pulling him down, her mouth lifting to his.

Sweet. *And hot.* He tangled a hand in her loose hair, keeping her close, turning his head for a better fit.

She made a soft sound and opened her mouth. He felt her tongue and gave her his own.

Scooping his other arm around her waist, he arched her into him. It wasn't enough, not when he wanted, needed, to be inside her again, hearing her fast breaths and small cries, feeling the clench of her body as she neared release…

Tires on gravel alerted them both and they jumped apart.

Lisa looked startled, her hair mussed, her lips swollen.

He blew out a breath. Damn it, he had a boner. "Stay put and I'll deal with it." Pulling his shirt out and down to cover himself, he headed for the building.

Her cousin Amber exited her truck with yet another man.

Jesus, where did she find all the guys? Did she recruit them from out of the county?

Pasting on a smile, he said, "Amber. Hi."

"Hey, Gray." She slid a look over him and gave a very knowing smile. "Dave and I were headed into town and I figured I'd stop to say hi to Lisa. Is she here yet?"

"I'm not sure," he lied, and eyed the guy.

"Dave and Lisa went to school together."

"Is that right?" Like he gave a shit? Why did Amber persist in throwing men at her cousin? If the men were that great, she should keep them for herself. "You live around here, Dave?"

"Next county over."

Well, hell. Amber was bringing them in!

"I'm here visiting my mom. I didn't know Lisa was back. And working here?" He laughed. "Hard to believe."

It occurred to Gray that Amber still watched him. Waiting for his reaction to that possible insult? Gray smiled again. "Pretty sure she could work anywhere she wants, but yeah, she's helping out."

Dave rubbed his hands together. "When do you expect her?"

Lisa came around the corner. She'd smoothed her hair and straightened that sexy top, but her lips still looked thoroughly kissed and damn, he wanted her.

Dave probably did, too, the dick.

"Hey, Dave," Lisa said. Just that, nothing more.

"Lisa!" He took a step forward, his gaze gobbling her up. "It's so great to see you. How've you been?"

"Busy." She kept walking, right past Dave and right up to her cousin, where she hooked her arm and began dragging her away. "If you guys will excuse us a moment?"

Amber looked back at Gray and laughed. In triumph? Sounded like.

Hands in his pockets, Gray eyed Dave. "So."

Dave kept staring after the women. "She looks good."

"Yeah."

"Last time I saw her, she was all buttoned up in a business suit."

Bet she looked sexy as hell, too. "When was that?"

"Few years ago. We were both out of town and ran into each other."

"Got to catch up?"

"Not really. She had a grueling schedule to keep."

Good.

The women returned. Lisa, utterly serene, said, "Dave, it was nice seeing you."

Confused by that dismissal, Dave said, "Uh..."

"I need to get to work now."

Amber kept grinning. "Come on, Dave. We don't want to hold them up." But as she opened her truck door she said to Gray, "So Sunday. Any chance you can get away?"

Lisa, whipping back around, lost her serenity. "Amber!"

Gray said, "Probably," and hoped like hell he didn't regret it. "I have a part-time guy who helps out when necessary."

Lisa blinked at him. "I didn't know that."

"He's been on a vacation to visit his brother in Texas, but he's due back Wednesday."

"Who?" Lisa demanded, which sort of tickled Gray. For a hotshot businesswoman, she'd really taken a territorial liking to her job at the marina.

"Petie Burkman." And from what Gray could tell, Petie was another veteran of the county. Everyone seemed to know him.

Sure enough, Lisa nodded. "He used to run the garage in town. He has to be in his seventies now."

"Almost his eighties, I think." Petie had the thickest white hair Gray had ever seen, a lot of wrinkles from overexposure to the sun and a lazy way of getting things done. But he was also trustworthy, sharp as a tack and reliable. "He came with the shop when I purchased it."

Lisa took that in, said, "Okay," as if it had needed

her approval and then rounded on her cousin again. *"Amber."*

Amber ignored her. "Two o'clock, okay, Gray? Join my family and me and I'll introduce you around, let everyone get to know you better. Lisa can show you where. I'll tell everyone to expect you."

Gray gave it very quick thought, saw Dave staring at Lisa's legs and said, "Sounds good, thanks. Can I bring anything?"

"Your swimming trunks and a smile." Amber practically stuffed Dave into the truck, then got behind the wheel and drove away.

Her dust hadn't yet settled before Lisa groaned. "I'm sorry."

"For?"

"Getting you shanghaied. I told her no more on the man parade and she apparently refocused on you. I should have expected it. Especially after..." Her voice trailed off and she touched her cheek.

Intrigued, Gray asked, "After?"

Lisa sighed and dropped her hand. "After she saw the whisker burn on my cheek."

He tipped her face up, saw the small pink mark and bent to kiss it gently. "She asked?"

"She's Amber. Of course she asked."

"What did you tell her?"

"I think I stared, stammered and then told her to take Dave away and cease with the matchmaking."

"Avoidance and deflection. Guess it didn't work?"

She huffed. "With Amber? Not ever."

"She means well." At least, that was the impression Gray got. Assuming the moment had passed and she was done making out with him, Gray went to the shop door and held it open for Lisa.

"Everyone encourages her, that's the problem." Grumbling, Lisa strode in past him. "Someone should meddle in her love life, let her see how it feels."

Love life? "My family is small, especially compared to yours." Gray figured every family might be small compared to hers. "So clue me in. You and Amber get along or not?"

"Of course! I love her—pushy faults and all." Heading to the coffeepot, she added, "And usually she's dead-on. I mean, Amber is the one who fixed up Shohn with Nadine, and she had a lot to do with Garrett and Zoey getting together."

After chugging down half the coffee, Lisa continued. "Rumor has it Amber even had a hand in Casey's romance with Emma, even though she was only a kid at the time."

"Sounds like she's good at what she does."

Lisa ignored his input. "But she's never been able to accept that I—"

This time her voice dropped like a stone in the lake. "That you what? Were too busy working to get interested?"

Deflated, she stared at the remaining coffee in her cup. "That I've never met anyone interesting enough to get interested."

So he was interesting enough? Because, damn, it sure felt like she was interested.

"Mmm," Lisa said around another drink of coffee. "How is it you do everything so well? Even your coffee is excellent."

"Lisa?"

She peeked at him and said, "What?"

"That kiss."

Her expression softened, her eyes going darker,

sultry—just as he remembered. "You did that really, *really* well."

Behind them a family walked in, chatting. When Gray glanced that way he saw the mom, the dad and even the kid were decked out in clichéd fishing gear, which meant they were novices, because all the seasoned fishermen knew better than to wear hats full of hooks.

With free time gone, he turned back to Lisa.

Those soul-sucking eyes of hers were steady on his face. "We were supposed to be getting to know each other better."

Gray nodded.

"But you're right. I know you." She closed the space between them, put a hand to his chest, and whispered, "I wish we'd had more time."

Well, damn. How was he supposed to work after she said that?

"You owe me a second cup." And with that she up-ended her coffee to finish it off, patted his chest and started for the family. Watching her sassy walk, it took a second before Gray grinned. He'd made headway.

So now all he needed was more time.

CHAPTER FOUR

HAD HE REALLY left the force for a slower pace? Didn't feel like it. The first three days of the second week with Lisa had been nothing short of insane. Vacationers flocked to the lake, and more than half of them had no clue about boating safety and lake regulations.

A bunch of college kids had shown up with a pontoon that they planned to drastically overload. The cop in him came out and he'd refused to let them launch—which had caused a scene with thirteen pissed-off college idiots who were already lit at ten in the morning.

Gray hadn't seen Lisa disappear, but a few minutes later her uncle Morgan, the freaking mayor, was there with the sheriff, and Gray had taken satisfaction in being able to back off and let others handle it.

Lisa did introductions immediately afterward. Gray liked the sheriff. Tucker Turley gave off a mild-mannered, won't-get-riled vibe that he quietly backed up with pure steel. It was actually entertaining to watch.

He also learned that her uncle, who had once been sheriff before being elected mayor, now headed up the COCP program, or Community Organized Crime Prevention. Made up of local agencies, which included Shohn as a ranger and Garrett as a firefighter, as well as area residents, the COCP coordinated to fight minor crime, delinquency, vandalism and such.

Nice that her uncle cared enough to stay so involved, and because of that he wielded a lot of respect and confidence.

Turley, much younger, had the badge but didn't seem to mind Morgan's input—which proved Turley was confident and smart. Better to work with Morgan than fight against him.

Being the authority figure, Gray knew, was hard to shake. It got in your blood, settled into your bones and stuck.

Just yesterday, early evening, some yahoo had decided to teach a ten-year-old kid how to swim by throwing him in without a jacket. He'd heard Lisa yell, a bigger splash, and seconds later she'd waded out with her arm protectively around the shaken kid, who was still coughing up lake water. Already headed toward them, Gray watched her gently seat the boy on a bench, then whirl in a fury on the man. She'd poked his chest, crowded into his space and snapped loud enough for everyone on the lake to hear, *"Are you an idiot?"*

With a lot of audacity, the guy had yelled back, "Mind your own damn business, lady!"

Gray hadn't remembered moving, but in a heartbeat he was between them, so pissed that breathing wasn't easy. Through his teeth, he'd growled, "Back it down. Now."

The guy had, but before Gray could say anything more a woman appeared. She was even more pissed than Gray. From what he could figure, the man was a disappointing blind date and the lady was already done with him. After chewing the guy up one side and down the other, she'd put a life preserver on her son, gotten him in the boat—which was apparently hers, not his—and she took off…leaving the man still on shore.

Smug, Lisa had watched him head for his car. When he'd realized he didn't have the keys, he launched into another fit. He'd even kicked the car.

Scowling, Lisa had headed for him, but Gray cut her off. "No." She tried to go around him, so he'd stopped her again. "I'll deal with it."

Gray had watched the hesitation in her eyes, then saw the trust. "Okay."

The confrontation hadn't gone well. The guy had blustered and shouted and caused a scene. Gray kept his cool.

Finally, with some vague threats, the man stomped off. Where he'd gone, Gray didn't know, but as long as he left, it didn't matter to him.

Lisa had smiled at him, patted his chest, and just that easily she'd gone back to helping other folks. When the woman and her son returned near dark, she'd taken the time to thank both Lisa and Gray. Blind dates, she declared, were off her agenda forever. She'd hugged her son, a cute little boy, and said she'd be back again. Gray and Lisa both waved her off, and they hadn't had a chance to talk about it since.

Luckily, the mishaps after that were simple ones, easily corrected. But he made a note to stock up on life preservers and to post a large sign sharing navigation rules and a required equipment chart.

Now here it was, the butt crack of dawn on the fourth day, and Gray, wearing running shorts and sneakers with a loose T-shirt and a backward ball cap, headed up the walk to Lisa's house. That she had a house didn't surprise him; she was a very resourceful, intelligent and capable woman.

But from what he understood, she hadn't stayed in Buckhorn much. Maybe the house meant that, deep down, she'd always intended to settle back home at some point.

He hoped so.

He'd gotten her address from Amber, who still stopped by the marina at least every other day but, thankfully, no longer dragged other dudes along. His plan was simple—spend more alone time with Lisa without pressuring her. From what Amber had said, Lisa got enough pressure from everyone else. Her massive family wanted her to put down roots, and they weren't shy in attempting to sway her.

For once the skies were cloudy and the air smelled of rain. He knew fishing boats would flock to the lake, but there'd be fewer skiers, and for today, at least, he liked that trade-off.

If he caught Lisa before her jog, he could join her. It wasn't an intimate dinner, and it was a far cry from sex, but at least they wouldn't have half the lake's population crowded around them.

Assuming what her brother and cousin had said was true, she jogged each morning. To do that, she'd have to already be up and about. And if she wasn't yet up and he woke her…maybe that'd be okay, too. Gray pictured her all drowsy and sleep rumpled and had to fight off a boner.

When he had his hand raised to knock on her front door, it suddenly opened and Lisa rushed out, almost plowing into him.

He caught her upper arms, then winced from her short, startled scream. "Hey, it's just me."

Wide-eyed, she blinked him into focus, then shoved him back and put a hand to her heart. "Gray! What in the world are you doing here? You scared me half to death."

He took in her fitted running clothes and felt the slow burn of desire. "I was hoping to jog with you."

The hand went from her heart to her high, sloppy ponytail. "But… I don't like anyone to see me like this. It's why I jog so early."

"It's just me."

Expression droll, she said, "You're at the top of the list of people who should never see me wrecked."

"You're not wrecked." Far from it. "The shorts are hot."

Her laugh teased over him as she looked down at her pink gym shorts. "Hot, huh?"

"Mostly because of the ass inside them. And the legs." He slid a hand to her waist. "And I could totally envy that sports bra."

"Envy?"

"It's holding your rack all snug."

Grinning, she stepped past him and pulled her door shut. "You realize that now you really do have to jog."

"You think I can't?" Did she consider him a slacker?

"With your bod?" She snorted. "I'm sure you aren't afraid of exercise."

"Actually, I like it." Before his leg injury he used to jog regularly. Anticipating the run, he looked around the dark neighborhood. "Where do you jog, anyway?"

"I start here, go up through the school yard, circle

around to the main street, then back. It only takes forty minutes or so."

"Thought you didn't want to be seen."

With a chuckle, she elbowed him. "This is Buckhorn, Gray, not the city. Other than the grocery, which now stays open overnight, the businesses don't open until ten, later on Saturday, and not at all on Sunday. The farmers will be up and about, but we won't see them. Uncle Morgan might be at the courthouse, and Uncle Gabe sometimes starts early if he has a lot to get done. Dad's vet clinic is farther out and Uncle Sawyer still works from home."

"Question—unless I misunderstood, your uncles are brothers, so why do they all have different last names?"

"Caught that, did you? Well, it's easy enough. Uncle Sawyer and Uncle Morgan are the oldest, and they're both Hudsons. Their dad died when they were really young and my grandma remarried and had my dad. But apparently things didn't work out and they divorced. He took off and Dad's never really known him. Then my grandma remarried again and had Uncle Gabe, and she and Grandpa Brett are still together."

"I haven't met her."

"They live in Florida but make it up here several times a year. Stick around and I'm sure you'll have the pleasure." Smiling fondly, Lisa headed for the sidewalk. "Grandma is something. A small, sweet dynamo."

"Sounds like someone else I know."

Brows angled, she asked, "Who?"

He laughed. "You."

"But I told you, we're not blood related."

"There are a lot of things more important than blood."

She thought about that a second, then nodded.

Gray followed her out to the sidewalk, filled his lungs with the clean, storm-thick air and stretched. "I like it here."

Gaze on his body, she said, "Me, too."

But did she like it for the long haul? He hoped so. "Your house is nice." Big enough for a family, but still cozy. Well-trimmed shrubs, flowering annuals and perennials brightened the midsized white ranch with a slate-gray roof and matching shutters. She had a big yard with a few mature trees and a really nice porch holding two rockers.

"Thanks. I bought it as an investment, you know? But since I've been back, I've done some decorating and now it feels more like mine."

"When?" She'd been working with him from sunup to sundown. Whenever he tried to give her a break, she refused.

"When what?"

"When would you have had time to decorate?" Sometimes he suspected she used the marina as a hide-out from her imposing and often demonstrative family.

Rather than answer, she started off at an easy lope. Gray held back, enjoying the view. Her ponytail bounced—as did her bottom. Her legs were strong but sleek. Her waist small. Her shoulders straight.

Not once did she look back for him, so he caught up and then metered his pace to match hers. He enjoyed the rhythmic slapping of sneakers on pavement, the way they fell into an easy cadence together. Lisa had a nice, even stride, long for her height.

"In the evenings," she said, not even a little breathless, "I do online shopping. It takes me a while to unwind when I get home, so whenever something new has arrived, curtains or wall art or whatever, I unpack it and put it up."

"I wouldn't mind helping you with that."

She just smiled. "Thanks."

Hell, he'd like to help her with anything, just to spend more time with her. "If you need time off, just tell me."

"I will." They went another block in silence before she spoke again. "I'm very undecided about so many things. It helps to stay busy."

A perfect opening. "I could help with that, too, without you being on the clock."

"Yeah?" She flashed him a grin. "What did you have in mind?"

Only half under his breath, he said, "If I told you everything on my mind, you'd probably slap me."

Eyes straight ahead, she said, "Doubtful, since it's on my mind as well."

"It?"

"Us." She peeked at him, then jogged across the street at a crosswalk in front of the middle school.

Gray caught up to her again. "Think we need to do anything about it?"

"Yes."

He stopped for a heartbeat, but Lisa didn't. Again he quickened his pace to rejoin her. He liked her profile, the very slight smile showing, how her long lashes left shadows on her cheeks. How her breasts jiggled a little despite being squished by the sports bra. "Okay, when?"

She kept going, pushing herself harder, but eventually said, "I like it that you want me. That you know a part of me no one else knows."

No one? Meaning no other guy? "I'm trying to be

patient, honey, you know that. Just know that it's not easy, okay?"

"Other women have made offers."

He shrugged. "Other men have made offers."

She shot him a look. "To you?"

Laughing, he shook his head. "To *you.*"

"Oh." She waved that off as if it didn't matter.

"Not interested?" he asked. "Not even a little?"

"Not even a little."

That was something, anyway. "Same here." He let that sink in, then added, "I want you. Only you." And for her, he was willing to wait. "Just so you know."

"You don't make it easy."

All's fair in love and war. "I'm pushing too much?"

She shook her head. "No, you're just too damned irresistible." Lengthening her stride, she tried to leave him, but he just grinned and kept pace and shortly, a little winded, she slowed again.

They entered the town, lit by stately lampposts lining the street. Weak rays of sunrise couldn't quite penetrate the heavy gray clouds. A light sprinkle started, sending steam to rise from the heated pavement. Lisa didn't mention it, so Gray didn't, either.

They passed an old-fashioned post office, a grocery, an ice cream shop. Lights shone inside the diner, but it wasn't yet open, and sure enough, her uncle Morgan had just pulled into the courthouse. Spotting them, he paused as he got out of his utility vehicle, then started toward them.

"He sees us," Gray told Lisa.

She kept her nose down and kept going.

"He's walking out to greet us."

"Pretend you don't see him," she muttered.

Yeah, right. A man of Morgan Hudson's size and presence would be impossible not to see. "Sorry, can't. It'd make me look both chickenshit and rude."

"Damn it." Slowing her pace, Lisa looked up and smiled brightly, as if only then seeing the big bruiser.

"Faker," Gray whispered.

"Hush." And then, louder, she said, "Uncle Morgan, hi."

Morgan gave his niece a double take and laughed. "The words are right, honey, but the inflection is off. I gather you were hoping to miss me?"

"No, of course not. I always enjoy seeing you."

"'Cept when you have a swain keeping pace?" Morgan slanted his attention to Gray.

Lisa said quickly, "I work for him."

"I know that. Also know Amber tried to fix you up a few times, but you weren't having it."

Lisa groaned.

Gray smiled and offered his hand. "Nice to see you again, Mayor."

Taking his hand, her uncle indulged in an easy greeting without any of the usual fist-crunching, pissing-contest nonsense. "Morgan'll do. 'Specially since Amber tells me you're joining us this Sunday."

"Yes, sir."

"I looked you up." Finally, Morgan freed his hand. "You were a damn good cop. Shame what happened. I see your leg is okay now?"

Aware of Lisa watching him, Gray stiffened. "I'm fine."

"Yeah, that's how I'd tell it, too." Morgan didn't leave. In fact, he scrutinized Gray. "I was especially sorry to read about your partner."

"Thank you."

Lisa half stepped in front of her uncle. "What happened to your leg?"

Gray pulled off his cap, ran a hand through his hair, then replaced it—this time facing forward. "It's nothing."

She rounded on Morgan. "Spill it."

"Not my story to tell, honey." Morgan caught her shoulders, held her still for a loud kiss on the forehead, then stepped back. "I'll let you two finish your jog. But Gray?"

Gray lifted a brow.

"Everyone's looking forward to Sunday. Don't chicken out."

Lisa groaned.

Gray stiffened even more. "Wouldn't miss it."

Laughing, Morgan said, "Yeah, I think you'll do."

Gray watched the mayor stride away because that was easier than meeting Lisa's curious gaze. "Ready to finish this jog?"

"Gray?" She touched his arm.

"You need a break?"

Sighing, she trailed her hand up his arm to his biceps, where she lingered a moment, then to his shoulder. Right there on the sidewalk in front of the courthouse with her uncle not that far away, she stroked over his chest. "This is one of those times where we could get better acquainted."

"Shit." He scrubbed a hand over his face. He didn't like talking about himself, not when talking about Lisa would be far more interesting. But she stood there with those mesmerizing dark eyes and he caved. "You didn't notice the scar on my thigh the night we got together?"

"You were naked," she said as if that explained it. "I was taking in the whole package."

He lifted a brow.

Face flushed, she said, "Not *that* package. I mean…" More color filled her cheeks. "I liked that, too."

Grinning, Gray folded his arms and gave her his undivided attention.

She huffed out a breath. "I liked all of it. Of *you*, I mean. Maybe…too much?"

Too much? Not possible.

Throwing up her hands, she said, "You're gorgeous. You know that. And your body…"

When she shivered, he felt it in his dick. "Any time you want a second showing, let me know."

"I think I do."

His heart tried to punch out of his chest. "Yeah?"

"Will you show me your leg?"

"Sure." Given the wound was high, damn near to his groin, he'd have to get naked, which suited him just fine. "My leg. Both legs. Top to bottom, yours to view. Or touch. Whatever you have in mind…"

Laughing, she swatted him but quickly sobered. "Come on."

He fell into a jog beside her.

"Will you at least tell me how it happened?"

He didn't want to. Hell, he hated talking about it. But given he wanted to know everything about her, it only seemed fair. "Yeah."

"When?"

"When I'm showing you my leg."

She laughed again. "Okay, then. How about tonight?"

He stopped. So did she.

Searching her face, he said, "Tonight works."

Her voice lowered, went as husky as his. "Okay."

Damn, she kept him wired. And confused. "Are we talking about *talking*, or—"

"Well, this looks serious."

They both jumped, turned as one, and found another of her relatives grinning at them through an open truck window.

Gray bit back his groan.

Lisa slapped on another false smile. "Uncle Gabe."

Gabe laughed. "Know what, Lisa? You sound just like I used to when Mom busted me." He eyed them both. "Planning some hanky-panky?"

"Uncle Gabe!"

"Hey, I'm told Gray is staying in Buckhorn, so if he's the lure that keeps you here, it's okay by me. Long as he's a nice guy." Expression changing, Gabe zeroed in on him. "You a nice guy, Gray?"

He didn't miss the warning in the question. "When being nice is appropriate, sure."

Gabe held his gaze for a few beats, then laughed. "I like him, honey. Carry on." Stepping on the gas, Gabe drove away.

"Can't walk a block without tripping over a damned relative."

Gray grinned at her. "They're protective."

"And gossipy, too. Gabe and Morgan will tell Dad and Sawyer and they'll all tell their wives and everyone in the entire family will think we have a thing."

Gray raised his hand. "Guilty." He had a thing all right. More than a thing. He just needed to get Lisa on board. But until she made up her mind about whether or not to stay in Buckhorn, he didn't want to put her on the spot.

Because he was staying.

Before she could ask all those questions he saw in her gaze, Gray said, "Now, about us getting together again." He brushed the backs of his fingers over her cheek. "I can have Petie close up tonight so we can both get off at seven. What do you think?"

"I think everyone in Buckhorn is going to know."

Probably. From what he could tell, word traveled fast. Challenging her, he asked, "How old are you?"

"Thirty."

"I'm thirty-two. That makes us both old enough to do whatever we damn well please."

Her breath shuddered out. "Oh, Gray." Eyes dark and heated and seductive, she whispered, "We pleased an awful lot."

Yeah, and it ate him up thinking about it. "Damn, baby. Don't look at me like that."

"Like what?"

"Like you're remembering everything and wanting a repeat. I can't get hard, not here on the street in running shorts." He cupped her face, tipped it up to his. "Now tell me we have a date regardless of who will know."

The lustful haze lifted with her smile. "It doesn't bother me if it doesn't bother you."

"Doesn't bother me even a little." All that mattered was having her again.

For the longest time she stared up at him, and finally she laughed. "You're a brave man, Gray Neely. Sexy, nice and brave. I hope you know what you're getting into."

CHAPTER FIVE

AROUND LUNCHTIME, when the shop finally cleared out, Lisa came over with the last few bites of a microwaved taco and a can of cola, and she hopped her sexy behind up onto the counter beside Gray. Which, of course, guaranteed he wouldn't get anything else done.

Today she wore actual cutoffs frayed along the very tops of her thighs and a sleeveless red blouse. His own adorable, hotter-than-hell country bumpkin.

As he pushed aside a few catalogs of summer gear, she asked, "My place or yours?"

He trailed one finger down her arm. "My place is closer."

Looking back at the door to the stairs, she asked, "How close?"

He pointed up to the ceiling.

She rearranged the wrapper on her taco to get the last bite. "Have you really thought this through?"

"Yes." No hesitation. He knew exactly what he wanted: her.

As if he hadn't spoken, she pointed out, "Because my family has noticed you. And that means they'll bring on the pressure and have all these expectations, and while I might not be here, you say you will be."

"Definitely." And he hoped she'd stick around, too.

As she'd said, her family was here. She had a house. Would that be enough?

"So do you really want to deal with that?"

He wanted to deal with her. "I'm a big boy. Don't worry about me."

"But—"

"Lisa." Leaving the chair, he walked around to stand in front of her. He took the empty wrapper from her hand and pitched it toward the garbage can.

She watched it land inside. "Good shot."

Gray set her Coke aside, then flattened his hands on the counter at either side of her hips. "You can't talk me out of what I want, but if it's not what you want, you can tell me. I'll deal with it."

She stared at his mouth. "I want you."

Much as he loved that, he asked, "But?"

"Everything is so complicated."

"Doesn't have to be."

Suddenly she put her arms around him and hugged him tight. "I don't want to leave you with a mess."

He wanted to say, *Then don't leave*. But he was determined not to push her on that. She needed to make her own decision—and he'd help by making Buckhorn more enticing.

Smoothing her hair, he said, "I can handle your family." He hoped.

She laughed and hugged him tighter. "Oh, you poor misguided man."

Okay, so he was being pretty optimistic about that. But he'd routinely handled petty thugs and hard-core criminals, prosecutors and defense attorneys, even stubborn-as-hell judges. How bad could her family be? "Trust me."

The air around them seemed to crackle. She snuggled closer, kissed his throat and said, "I think I always have."

That did it for him.

Giving her time to object, Gray slowly parted her thighs and stepped between them, then, with his hands on her trim hips, he snugged her up close so their bodies meshed.

"Gray," she whispered before melting against him.

"Damn." He kissed her throat, her shoulder, over to her jaw.

Hands tight on his shoulders, she sought his mouth with hers. When their lips touched, they both went still, but not for long. Sinking a hand into her hair, Gray kept her close and nudged her lips open, turned his head for a better angle, sank his tongue in to taste and tease. *This.* He'd needed this a lot. But only with her.

The kiss went hot and wet and deep. But it wasn't enough, not even close. The better he knew her, the more he thought forever wouldn't be enough. She gave a soft groan, arched into him—

A noise sounded behind them.

Taken off guard—something that never happened—Gray jerked around, blocking her with his body. What he saw left him blank.

Not customers. No one from her family.

Just a stray dog.

Relieved that he hadn't let Lisa get caught in a compromising situation that might've embarrassed her, Gray took in the ancient dog peeking into the shop with eyes almost as dark as Lisa's. Half covered in mud, a rough rope tied around his neck, he looked miserable.

And that got Gray pissed really quick.

Breathing hard behind him, unaware of the dog, Lisa whispered, "Oh, God."

"Shh," he told her. "It's a stray dog."

Immediately her head popped up over his shoulder. "Ohhh," she whispered. "The poor baby. Is he hurt?"

"I don't know, but he's not in good shape." Hearing them, the animal started to slink away, so Gray said to her, "Stay here."

"What are you going to do?"

"Check on him, if I can." Help him, if at all possible. "C'm'ere, boy. You okay? Scared, huh. I bet." He kept his voice low and made painstaking progress at getting closer. The rope around the animal's neck looked too damned tight, like a cruel trick. He'd seen a lot of shit in his lifetime, but anything involving animals or kids really did him in.

He heard Lisa moving behind him, and a second later he felt her touch on his back. "Offer him this."

He took the beef jerky and held it out.

The dog went on alert, ears up, nose sniffing the air.

Chances of getting bitten seemed good, so Gray tossed a piece toward the dog.

He caught it in the air and swallowed it in one gulp.

Yeah, that rope dug into the dog's neck, way too tight. Gray tossed another bite, making this one closer so the dog had to step farther inside while Gray circled to the side. He kept it up, wanting to get behind the dog so he could close the door.

But first… "Lisa, I need you to go up to my place. If the dog freaks out, I don't want you to get bit."

"No."

Since he'd given that order in his best cop voice, he stalled. "This isn't—"

"Hush, Gray." Phone to her ear, she said, "Hey, Dad, it's me. We need a little bit of help. I don't suppose you have any free time?" Quickly she explained the situation, and when she disconnected, she said, "He's on his way."

What the hell? Did she think her dad could do something he couldn't?

"He's a vet," she reminded him. "And we're in luck. He was using today for house calls, so he's not that far away. Fifteen minutes, he said. Instead of trying to trap the dog, let's just keep feeding him. Once he's here, Dad will know what to do."

It wasn't in Gray's nature to ask for help, but Lisa seemed to have no problem with it. At least when the help came from her family.

"All right," Gray agreed. "Find some more food. But I don't want you near him."

Instead of taking exception to that, she said, "Gray? Is that a note tied to the dog's neck?"

He'd already seen it, so he only nodded. "Yeah." And far as he was concerned, whoever had put it there needed his ass kicked.

CHAPTER SIX

HER DAD GOT there in under ten minutes, and he had both Uncle Sawyer and Nadine, Shohn's fiancée, with him.

As her dad worked his magic, talking soothingly to the dog and quickly earning his trust, Lisa whispered, "Nadine owns a pet hotel, so she's really great with animals, too."

Beside them, arms crossed as he watched, her uncle Sawyer said, "Jordan has a way with animals."

Gray looked impressed. "He whispered and the dog just came to him. Like he knew him or something."

"They all do that with Dad."

Nadine nodded. "I've seen him whisper to cows and goats and hawks and groundhogs. They all love him."

The exaggeration, slight as it might be, made Lisa grin, especially since it looked as though Gray believed her. Her grin died, however, once the rope was off the dog and they saw the note.

Jordan handed it off to Nadine, who read it and then handed it to Sawyer. "*'You'll pay,'*" he read. And then to Gray, "Any ideas?"

"Yeah. A cruel idiot." Seeing Jordan had it under control, Gray joined him, going down on his haunches to cautiously stroke the marks left around the dog's throat. "He'll be okay?"

"She, but yes."

"She?"

Lisa grinned again at Gray's expression. "A girl, Dad?"

"Yes, and by the looks of her, I'd say she's at least twelve, maybe older. A mutt, but I see a lot of coonhound in her. She's malnourished, has some small wounds that need attention, and she needs a good cleaning." He looked at Gray. "If it's okay with you, I'd like to take her in and get her treated."

"Please," Gray said. "Do whatever she needs and then let me know what I owe you." He again stroked the dog, and this time she tipped her head up, her eyes closed as if relishing the touch.

Lisa understood that; she often felt the same when Gray put those warm, strong hands on her.

Nadine nudged her, and she realized both her dad and Uncle Sawyer were watching her. Clearing her throat, she asked Gray, "Do you plan to keep her?"

"Yes."

No hesitation. She really liked that about him. Decisive. Caring. "I'm glad."

Her dad got a crate from the back of his truck. "If I'd known I'd be bringing one back with me," he said, "I'd have lined it with something soft."

"Here." Just like that, Gray pulled off his T-shirt and handed it over.

Neither her dad nor her uncle seemed to think anything of it, but once Lisa got her eyes to blink she noticed that Nadine was staring with rapt surprise.

It was Lisa's turn to offer a nudge.

Nadine turned to her and silently mouthed, *Wow.*

Nodding, Lisa agreed with her.

"I understand she'll be fine with you," Gray was saying to her dad. "But I feel bad just letting her go."

"Then don't." Uncle Sawyer, avoiding her gaze, stepped in. "Sheriff Turley's going to need to see that note."

"I'll handle it," Gray said with silky menace.

"All the same, Turley needs to know. I'm free today, Jordan's free, and I'm sure Lisa can handle the shop for a few hours."

Seeing a trap closing in, Lisa said, "But—"

"Ride back with us," Sawyer continued. "After we talk to the sheriff, I can show you Jordan's clinic. It'll give us a chance to get better acquainted."

Her dad gave her a look, then said to Gray, "We'll need to fill out some paperwork for her. On the way to the clinic, you can think up a name."

The dog, after sniffing the shirt Jordan spread in the crate, went in willingly.

"She's smart," Nadine said. "If there's anything you need from me, let me know. Otherwise I think I'll hang out and give Lisa a hand."

Again, Lisa tried to protest.

But Gray beat her to the punch, asking, "Do you mind?" His eyes, the color of the stormy sky, stared into hers. "I'll be back before we're due to close."

He might as well have said, *In time to give you everything I promised with that hot, killer kiss.*

The dog watched her, so how could she refuse? Deflated, Lisa flapped a hand. "It's been a slow day, what with the rain. Go on. I'm sure we'll be fine."

Grinning, probably anticipating a lot of girl talk, Nadine said, "This is going to be fun."

Gray said, “Let me grab another shirt and I’ll be right with you.” He disappeared inside.

Lisa stood there, her father, uncle and Nadine all watching her. She chose to focus on the dog. “Such a sweetie. How long will you need to keep her?”

“If there’s nothing major wrong, I can give her back to you at the picnic Sunday.”

“Back to Gray, you mean.”

Her dad just gave her another long look.

Luckily Gray returned, still buttoning up his short-sleeved cotton shirt. He paused beside her, said, “I won’t be long,” and right there, in front of family and a friend, he put his mouth to hers.

Lisa was so shocked she didn’t even blink.

Smiling, he touched her cheek. “You have my number if anything comes up.” He kissed her again, then strode to the dog crate and, like freaking Superman, put his hand in the handle and lifted it as if it didn’t hold a large dog.

Sawyer grinned back at Lisa. “I like him.”

Brows up, her dad opened the back of the truck. “Yeah.”

When Gray said, “I’ll ride back here with her,” Nadine put a hand to her heart and whispered, “Oh, me, too.”

Amazing. Gray had told her he could handle her family. She’d had her doubts, but wow, he’d just made it look pretty easy.

They were all won over.

And if she were honest with herself, she’d admit she wasn’t far behind them.

TUCKER TURLEY DIDN'T like the note, or the treatment of the dog, any more than Gray had, but as he'd already known, a note wasn't much to go on.

"Could've been meant for anyone," the sheriff said.

"Yeah," Gray agreed. But he trusted gut instincts, and his gut said the dog had been sent to him, specifically.

Which meant the lame *You'll pay* was a direct threat. So someone had a beef with him? He'd gotten along fine with all the locals, so he didn't have a clue.

They left with Tucker promising he'd keep both an eye and ear out. Neither Sawyer nor Jordan looked happy. And he knew why.

After they reached the clinic, Gray hovered nearby while Jordan checked the dog from nose to tail. He gave her some pain meds that he said would also make her sleepy. He put ointment on the raw abrasions on her neck, cleaned out her ears, checked her teeth and decided to let her eat and get a good night's sleep before bathing her in the morning.

After all that, they got the dog settled in a roomy kennel area, and Jordan said, "Let's get some coffee in the break room."

Which Gray knew was a euphemism for *Let us grill you to our satisfaction.*

He started the conversation by saying, "Hell of a nice setup you have."

"Thanks." Jordan filled three disposable cups, then pulled out a seat and sank into it. "Any thoughts on a name?"

"Yeah." Gray sipped his coffee, knew the men were analyzing him and said, "Shelby."

"Interesting choice," Sawyer said.

Shrugging, Gray explained, "My deceased partner's last name."

Clearly they already knew his background, given their quiet nods of respect. After a stretch of time, Jordan set his coffee aside. "Are you going to convince my daughter to stay in Buckhorn?"

Gray didn't deny that they had a relationship beyond employer and employee. Neither of these men was blind or stupid.

And of course, they'd witnessed the very deliberate, possessive kiss he'd given her.

But he wouldn't mind using the opportunity to get a point across. "I don't want to pressure her. All of you are doing enough of that."

Sawyer and Jordan shared a frown.

"What I will do," Gray said, "is give her plenty of reasons to stay."

The frowns smoothed out and the men grinned. As if remembering himself, Jordan coughed his away. "Lisa is—"

"Very special. I know."

Jordan agreed. "She's smart, and she can take care of herself. But if you have some nutcase after you, is it safe?"

"You don't have to worry." Gray knew well the dangers that existed in the world. "Whatever the note meant, no matter what the threat might be, I won't let anything happen to her."

After quietly taking that in, Sawyer asked, "You're armed?"

"At the shop, yes. Going forward, I will be everywhere." He hoped they understood that for a cop, carrying was second nature. "But even without a gun, I'd protect her."

Sawyer smiled. "Even though he's mayor now, Morgan says he feels naked without his gun."

"True story." Gray liked the familiar feel of the weapon, whether in a hip holster or at the small of his back. "Once a cop, always a cop."

Jordan said, "He told us about your partner. That had to be tough."

Sawyer tipped his head, his attention on Gray's leg. "You're okay now? Have full mobility back?"

"I'm fine." Gray saw the questions they didn't ask. Might as well clear the air now. He spent the next hour or so talking, and in the process he learned that he liked Sawyer and Jordan both. They were interested without being overly intrusive. Protective of Lisa while also showing their respect and insisting they trusted her to make the decisions best for her.

As a doctor, Sawyer asked plenty of questions about Gray's injury. Jordan had a quieter way about him, but Gray thought it might be deceptive, a way to hide the intensity.

They were good men, and he was glad Lisa had them in her life.

Before they left the clinic, Gray again checked on Shelby. Now that she'd been fed and had some meds, she was resting peacefully on a plush doggy bed—and his shirt. He stroked her, enjoyed the thumping of her tail and promised her he'd see her again in the morning. She closed her eyes on a big doggy yawn, so Gray didn't linger.

The later it got, the fewer people would be at the marina and the better the chance of Lisa being alone.

By the time Jordan dropped Gray back at the shop, it was raining again. Thanks to a call, they knew Nadine had left half an hour ago because business was so slow. Gray saw a man using the ramp to take a boat out. Along the shore, only two people, a woman and a man, cast out lines, their hats and windbreakers the only sign that they noticed the weather.

"Thanks again," Gray said to Jordan.

"You know, the previous owners sometimes closed up early on days like this. You could do the same."

Seeing Lisa in the doorway waiting on him, Gray decided that wasn't a bad idea. "Sounds like a plan." He opened the door and stepped into the downpour.

"Gray?"

He ducked his head back into the open truck door.

"Don't make me regret liking you."

Grinning, Gray closed the door and jogged to the shop. Soon as he reached the door, Lisa stepped back. She looked both worried and anxious and, damn, he wanted her.

Standing there, dripping on the floor, Gray looked her over. There seemed to be a sort of leashed tension in her small body. He saw her hands shaking, the shallow way she breathed. "Any problems?"

"No."

Hoping for the best, he asked, "Miss me?"

"Yes."

He drew a breath and went for broke. "I want you, Lisa. Right now."

As if that galvanized her, she rushed to the door, slammed and locked it.

Gray watched her, his heart racing, already getting hard.

Shooting to the window next, she turned the Open sign to Closed, then pulled the curtains so no one could see in.

"In a hurry?" he asked, so turned on he couldn't draw a deep breath.

"Yes." She headed past him for the door to the stairs. "Come on."

Snagging her hand as she passed, Gray pulled her back. "Just a second." Suffering his own urgency, he got his gun and keys from a drawer beneath the counter. Lisa didn't balk at the gun. She didn't even look all that surprised by it.

Stepping back, she let him unlock the stairs door and, after he relocked it with them on the other side, followed him at a more sedate pace up to his living area. Once there, Gray put the gun and keys on the table in the small kitchen, then stripped off his soaked shirt and draped it over a chair.

Lisa made a sound, stepped up against him, her hands on his chest, and a second later she went to her tiptoes to kiss him.

No longer caring that he was soaked through, Gray gathered her closer, his hands going down her slim back, cupping under her bottom, the backs of her thighs, back up again. Her hands were the same, sliding down his back to his shorts, then back up to curve over his shoulders.

He felt the sting of her nails and she practically tried to crawl into him.

He pressed her back enough to get the buttons on her blouse open, but he needed to kiss her, too, and soon they were tangled again. Once he got the top buttons undone, he managed to pull the blouse up and over her head.

No bra.

Breathing hard, he held her back and looked at her.

The frayed cutoffs fit low on her hips, showing off the slight curve of her belly, the dip of her waist, all that smooth, soft, pale peach skin. The shorts, faded and worn in spots, were about the sexiest thing he'd ever seen on a woman.

On this woman, they all but destroyed him.

Traveling upward, his hungry gaze took in her round, firm breasts. Excitement had drawn her nipples tight. His lungs constricted, his hands naturally lifting to cover her, to tease those stiffened nipples with his thumbs. A groan rumbled from deep in his chest.

At the same time, Lisa purred, her hands covering his.

"You're as beautiful as I remember."

When she started to kiss him, he whispered, "I want to see all of you," and reluctantly pulled his hands away. Taking a step back, he reached for the snap of her shorts. It opened easily and, taunting himself and her, he slowly dragged down the zipper.

Lisa stood there shivering with need, her attention on his face, seeing everything he felt. And he felt a lot.

With her shorts open, he put both hands inside the back, cuddling her cheeks for a moment and then sliding both her panties and her shorts down. Once past her thighs they dropped to her feet.

So sweet. And so fucking pretty. All over.

"Gray?"

He smoothed her hair behind her shoulders and just looked at her. He could look at her for a lifetime. He knew it, had felt it almost from the moment they'd met. She was his, now and always. The trick would be in getting her to want the same thing.

"Your turn," she said, lifting one hand to tease at the drawstrings to his shorts.

"No problem." He shucked off his remaining clothes in record time, then made her squeal when he scooped her up and headed for his bedroom. "Kiss me."

She did, and damn, but her kisses were hotter than sex with other women. She scorched him, especially with the hot way her tongue played with his, how her bare breasts felt on his chest, the way her fingers dug into his shoulders as she tried to hold him tighter.

At the side of the bed, he sank down with her small body tucked under his. She slid one leg up and around his hip, both her hands easing up to tangle in his hair while they indulged in a deep, eating kiss that left each of them panting.

Needing more, Gray nibbled a damp path down her throat to her breasts. He already knew she had extremely sensitive nipples, and he loved it. He started with a few licks, then sucked on her until she groaned. Carefully, he caught her pebbled nipple in his teeth and tugged.

"Gray."

Taking turns at each breast, he enjoyed her until she was crying out, her head back, her body moving rhythmically against his.

Wanting to see her come, he stroked a hand down her side, over that cute belly and between her legs, where he found her hot and already wet.

"Yeah," he rasped low, slicking his fingers over her, then in her to press deep.

She said his name on a high, thin cry.

Watching her, he brought his fingers out, up to her clitoris, then back in, pumping two or three times, then teasing her clit again. Over and over. She found his rhythm, her hips rolling, her throaty groans coming faster.

He licked over her already wet nipples, sucked insistently, and far too soon she started coming.

Gray held her, stayed with her, wrung her out until her hoarse cries faded and she went limp on the bed, eyes closed, lips parted.

Seeing her like that, sated by him, left protective, possessive urges surging through him. Even knowing it was too soon, he wanted to declare himself. Time wouldn't change anything for him, but hopefully it would for her.

Odd, but now that he had her here in his bed, he no longer felt the churning rush to get inside her. Instead he took immense pleasure in cuddling her, kissing her, touching her in soft, easy strokes over her waist, her shoulder, along her hip and thigh.

After a time, she sighed deeply, smiled a little. "I needed that."

"Mmm." He nuzzled her shoulder, breathed in her scrumptious scent and took a lazy bite. "Me, too."

With a husky laugh, she pressed at his chest. "That took the edge off, but I need more."

"A lot more." Sitting up, he snagged a condom from the bottom drawer of the nightstand. As he rolled it on, he felt her hand on his back, idly touching him. He turned, kneed her legs apart and settled over her. "Hi."

Her eyes, all warm, dark and mysterious, smiled at him. "Hi."

Adjusting, he moved against her, watched her face and sank in.

"Gray," she moaned.

Doing his utmost to maintain control, he began rocking into her, deeper each time, until their bodies were in perfect tune. It was all familiar, irresistible and yet still new because now he knew her, really knew her. And loved everything about her. "I enjoy hearing you say my name."

Opening her eyes and staring up at him, she whispered, "Gray."

"Tease." Her body squeezed around his cock, wetter and hotter. Ducking his face into her neck, he opened his mouth against her fragrant skin.

"I like teasing you." Her legs lifted around him and she locked her ankles at the small of his back. Near his ear she whispered, "Harder." And as he complied, she lifted into him, saying again, *"Gray."*

Damn. Her teeth caught his shoulder, she cried out, and this time, unable to stop himself, Gray came with her.

Sometime later he became aware of Lisa toying with his chest hair. He hugged her, kissed her forehead and rolled to his back.

She immediately moved over him.

Liking that, he murmured, "Nice."

"I don't want you to get too far away."

"Yeah?" Smiling, feeling more relaxed than he had in…well, a month, he settled a hand on her bottom. "Stay over and I promise to keep you within touching distance all night long."

Surprise widened her eyes, then she flushed. "I wasn't hinting."

"I know. I want you here." More than that, he *needed* her close. "Stay."

For only a moment she thought about it. "Okay." As she snuggled in, she said, "It'll give us a chance to talk."

Biting back his groan wasn't easy, but Gray managed it and even sounded casual when he asked, "Talk about what?"

She rose up to her elbows. "You. Your partner." Her hand went down his body to the top of his thigh—dangerously close to his junk—and settled over the scar. "And how you got this."

CHAPTER SEVEN

TEN MINUTES LATER, Lisa found herself sitting at Gray's kitchen table wearing one of his shirts and nothing else while he walked around in snug boxers and nothing else, making them sandwiches.

"I named the dog Shelby, after my partner, Vic Shelby."

Lisa sipped a glass of sweet tea and watched Gray. Just looking at him was wonderful. Long, leanly muscled thighs sprinkled with dark hair. Flat abs sporting that incredibly sexy happy trail. And his chest and shoulders...

Looking at him melted her bones and made her skin too tight and stirred that insanely hot, sweet lust to life again.

It swelled her heart to know he would finally open up to her, and the combo of lust and tenderness nearly did her in.

"I like the name."

"Good, because I'm keeping Shelby. I'd planned to get a dog after I got settled in anyway. She's such a sweetheart, and some coward used her to send me that note."

"And keeping her is the least you can do because you feel responsible?"

Turning his back to her as he sliced a tomato, he lifted a shoulder. "That covers it."

His back was as amazing as the rest of him. And that tight butt…but it was his big heart that really got to her. "Aww."

He scoffed at that. "Like I said, I wanted a dog anyway." He glanced back at her. "You don't mind?"

"One thing you should know about my family, we're very pet friendly. I didn't have a dog or cat because I traveled all the time. But I love animals."

"And now that you're here?"

She knew he deliberately left that open-ended. Unlike everyone else in her life right now, Gray didn't push. He made his intentions known, and he was real up-front about wanting her. But that was as far as he took it. She appreciated that a lot. "Now that I'm here, I'd be happy to help with Shelby." And maybe, if she ended up staying, she'd get a dog, too, a companion for Shelby. Or maybe a cat. She'd have to think about it.

"Now, about you and your partner and that wound that nearly unmanned you?"

"It was close, but luckily missed the vital parts."

Very close. The scar, a jagged line, cut across the top of one thigh. Healed now, thank God, but what if it had been a few inches over? Worse, what if it had been a killing blow?

Gray studied her, then went back to the sandwich prep. "So one day Shelby—my partner—and I were checking out a domestic dispute. A neighbor had called about the noise, said she heard a lot of angry arguing. From the second we got there, I knew it was going to be bad. There were three men and one woman and tensions were already so high, no one was listening. Some scumbag had hit his wife, and her two brothers were there to defend her. The husband and one of the brothers had felony records, everyone was ramped up on adrenaline and rage, and before we could even ask any questions, shit went south in a big way."

Gray had stopped moving. He had a butter knife in one hand, a piece of bread in the other, but he just… stood there. He seemed lost in the memory. A very ugly memory, given the strain in his broad shoulders.

Leaving her seat, Lisa walked over to him. She gently took the butter knife and bread and finished spreading the mayonnaise. "That's when you got hit?"

He pinched the bridge of his nose and put his head down. "Shelby took one to the chest and went down fast. I tried to cover him, but it felt like everyone was shooting, me, the two brothers, the husband…"

She leaned into him but didn't look right at him. She sensed how personal and painful this still was for him. "I can't imagine how devastating that must've been."

"We're trained," he said. "But there'd been no prior indication we were walking into a fucking war zone. The entire time we were shooting, the lady screamed—until she wasn't anymore."

Hurting for him, Lisa swallowed hard, tears clogging her throat.

"I was crouched over Shelby, covering him the best I could, and I got off some good shots. Hit one of the brothers and her husband, but the other dude ran off. The woman was already dead. Blood was literally everywhere, soaking Shelby, all over me…"

Suddenly he caught himself. She heard him taking deep breaths, saw his hands clench and unclench. After a low, nearly inaudible curse, he turned and leaned on the counter, watching her.

Lisa did her best to look…not devastated. But in her mind she saw it all and her heart wept for him. In a very short time, he'd come to mean a great deal to her. She couldn't bear the thought of him hurting, and yet he'd almost died.

Quietly, she finished the sandwiches and cut them into halves.

"You're pretty good at this," he finally said.

The lump in her throat almost strangled her, but she managed to keep things light. "At finishing up almost-finished sandwiches?"

"At listening." His warm, somber gaze went over her. "And looking good while doing it."

She gestured at his shirt, which she wore. "What? This old thing? I just threw it on."

Smiling, Gray pulled her in close for a kiss and then just held her, his arms around her, his chin on the top of her head.

"You're okay?"

"Yeah." He squeezed her. "The bullet to my thigh just grazed me. At the time I didn't even feel it. It wasn't until the paramedics showed up and told me I'd been hit that it started to hurt like a son of a bitch." He quieted, and Lisa waited, her arms around him, her cheek to his chest, listening to the steady thump of his heart. "The woman and one of her brothers were dead. Her husband, wounded, didn't put up much resistance after that. They found her other brother within ten minutes."

"Your partner was already gone?"

"No." Gray's hands contracted on her. "He held on for three long weeks. Seeing his wife go through that—I think that might've been the hardest part. We all knew he wouldn't make it, that we were leaning on false hope. But you can't help yourself."

"No."

"I'd just left the funeral when I met you."

She kissed his bare chest, then his shoulder, then went on tiptoe to reach his chin and finally his mouth. "I'm very, very glad you survived, Gray Neely."

Smoothing back her hair, looking at her, really looking at her, Gray nodded. "Me, too. Though I spent a hell of a lot of time wallowing in guilt because of it."

"I wish you wouldn't."

"That's the thing." He cupped her face, his expression serious. "I waffled between guilt and rage and being just plain numb. I wasn't sure what I wanted to do, or where I wanted to do it. But that night with you, I finally *felt* again. Everything. All good stuff. I thought I'd never see you again, and I hated that, but I woke that next morning knowing I would start fresh."

"In Buckhorn."

"Random shot in the dark, babe. I was checking around for something different and saw the ad for the marina."

"That's certainly different."

"But you know what?"

Since he was smiling now, Lisa smiled, too. "What?"

"I think it was fate." Scooping his hands under her bottom, he lifted her up and stepped to the wall, gently pinning her in place. His voice went husky and his lips almost touched hers. "I think we're good together."

Though she told herself that her plans were still up in the air, her heart tried to dance out of her chest. "I think so, too." Until Gray, sex was something she could take or leave, and usually she left it in favor of other, more exciting things—like wrapping up a new deal or finishing a business project. Now, well, she was starving but she'd gladly forgo the sandwiches if he wanted to take her right now. She couldn't imagine anything that could take her away.

In that moment, there was nothing she wanted more than Gray.

And from the look in his eyes, she thought he might be feeling the same.

"No pressure," he whispered. "I want you. Just about every way there is."

Wait—*what was he saying?*

"But if you decided tomorrow to go back to your old job, I'd still be here in Buckhorn."

"Um…okay?"

He smiled. "I want you to understand. You don't need to feel responsible for what we do or don't do, or how it might turn out. I like it here. I like your family, seeing the people who fish or swim or ski, the rowdy kids everywhere, and I like the lake. The broiling sunshine. The damp wind. All the birds and the frogs and turtles. All of it. I'm guessing I'll even like the winter, when everything is frozen and white and I'll be able to loaf around and put my feet up."

It wasn't easy to think because, really, he'd pinned her with his hips, which meant she felt his very noticeable erection. And he'd said he wanted her in *every way there is.* Confusing, to say the least—like, did he mean he wanted her beyond the physical, or maybe long-term?

All that, along with the scent of his warm body and the way he watched her with those stormy gray eyes—well, none of it was conducive to clear thought.

So she nodded.

That made his smile widen. "You have enough pressure, honey. You won't get it from me. Know that I want you, but if you want something different, I'll deal with it. That's all I'm saying."

Instead of giving her a chance to come up with a reply, or even to decide how she felt about his blithe attitude, he leaned in for a kiss, warm and soft, moving over her lips until she sighed. And maybe squirmed against him a little.

Her thoughts dissolved, her only focus on his mouth and how he tasted and how perfectly he worked those deliciously sculpted lips against hers. But as he started to trail kisses down her throat, she thought of something he'd said. "Wait."

"Okay."

She gasped for air, shook her head to clear the fog and caught his intent expression. "So." One more necessary breath and she felt clearer minded. "You plan to take the winters off?"

"Shocking idea for you, huh?" He kissed the end of her nose, as if her astonishment was...cute. "I like the idea of working hard all summer, relaxing during the worst months in the winter. I'm thinking spring and fall will still bring in some business, right?"

Could he afford to just take off for months at a time? How much did cops make anyway? Surely not—

As if he'd read her mind, he put his forehead to hers. "I bought the house and business outright. I'm thirty-two and single, and I was always frugal, so I had decent savings. Add that to the profit I made when I sold my house, which had been a fixer-upper, and it was easy enough. All I'm paying on is my boat."

Lisa sifted through everything he'd said, wondering why he'd told her about his financial status. But mostly she focused on one particular thing. She pushed him back to see him. "You have a boat?"

"You haven't noticed it sitting out back?" Mouth twisting, he added, "Still on a trailer?"

Of course she'd seen it, but…there were a lot of boats sitting around the lot. In fact, that was probably partial income in the winter, storing boats in a secure place. "You have a boat."

"Fishing poles, too." He shrugged. "Seemed necessary, with me buying a marina and all."

"A boat." Why hadn't she realized? "Well, we need to put it in."

Very slowly, he grinned, then nudged his erection at her. "With you so far."

Her face went hot. "Not *that*." What was she saying? Backtracking, she corrected, "Okay, that, too." He leaned in for another kiss, but she dodged him this time. "I meant your boat. Have you been out on the lake?"

"Once, before I bought this place." He got comfortable—pressed tight to her. "The previous owner took me around."

She gave it some thought. "How many hours do you plan to give to Petie?"

Gray shrugged, and as usual she enjoyed the flex of his strong shoulders. He held her up, between the wall and his body, with ease. "Now that he's back for the rest of the season, I was thinking a few hours each evening, Monday through Thursday, then half a day on Sunday."

"Perfect." She could work with that. "What about me?"

He put soft, damp bites on her neck. “When I get off, I want you to get off.”

The toe-curling way he teased distracted her, but to be sure, she asked, “Are we talking about work?”

“That, too.” Grinning, he lifted his head and kissed her mouth. “I want us to have a few evenings together, and Sunday afternoons, too.”

He’d already been thinking about it? Planning for more time with her? That deserved a big hug, which she gave him. “You’re an excellent planner.”

“Know what I’m planning now?”

Her heart skipped a beat and she whispered, “Tell me.”

“I’m planning to eat a sandwich.”

“Gray!”

He smooched her again. “With you.” Slowly he lowered her to her feet. “Then a shower.”

She frowned.

Until he said, “With you.”

Now that sounded better.

“And then I want to go back to bed—”

“With me?”

He nodded. “And I’m going to love you head to toes, and all those hot places in between, until you give me some of those sexy moans and sighs again, and then I’m going to hold you all night. What do you think?”

Lisa smiled dreamily. “Sounds like the perfect plan to me.”

SHELBY CAME HOME midmorning the next day. Jordan delivered her, then hung around a few minutes to ensure she was comfortable and to go over some meds with Gray.

Looking very uncertain, the dog sniffed around, wary of everyone but hungry for affection. Gray admired her now, after her bath and with her fur brushed. "She's beautiful."

"Mostly a bluetick coonhound," Jordan said, "but a mix for sure. Smart and gentle. I'm guessing at least ten years old, maybe older. I don't think she's at all aggressive, but keep an eye on her, okay?"

"I'm sure we'll get along just fine." Gray was careful to stroke her gently, especially around her abraded neck, taking care not to move too fast.

The rest of the day Shelby mostly slept, and the day after that she ate and slept, and the day after that she strolled out to the docks to laze in the sun—until kids showed up, then she lazed inside…and slept.

From what he could tell she didn't have a single aggressive bone in her body. If anything, she was too timid. But at her age, and having been neglected, it made sense that she might be uncertain.

Every so often, if Gray sat long enough, Shelby would come over and stare at him, then lean on his leg. He quickly learned that was his cue to pet or scratch or just give affection. She'd tip up her face, close her eyes, and it looked as though she smiled.

She showed no interest in getting on the furniture and chose to sleep alone at night, which was a good thing since she snored. Loudly.

The first time he heard it was only a few hours after he'd made love with Lisa. They both should have been sleeping, but the noise kept him awake. He'd come up on an elbow to look at Lisa.

Eyes open, she said, "Don't even think to blame me."

He grinned. "It's the dog."

"Yeah." Lisa smiled, too. She'd fallen fast and hard for Shelby, and did her best to pamper the dog. For the most part Shelby let her. "Guess we should get used to it."

That simple statement had affected Gray, because it was an indication that she planned to stick around. And thinking that stirred him, so it was an hour later before they got back to sleep. And he'd held Lisa close all night.

Each and every night, Lisa stayed over. She always wanted him to talk, so he did, but she didn't enjoy sharing about herself. She especially didn't want to talk about her job or whether or not she'd be staying in Buckhorn. So he didn't ask.

Everything he learned about her was from experiencing her, and paying close attention. Not a problem, since Lisa fascinated him.

When it came to Shelby, she seemed to have a sixth sense and just knew when the dog needed her. Like the time a woman came in with her little snapping dog that yapped incessantly and had Shelby backed up with her scruff starting to rise.

Suddenly Lisa was there, kneeling by Shelby, soothing her while glaring daggers at the lady. Gray scooped up her little ankle biter, got bitten in the process and nicely requested that the woman keep the dog on a leash, or carry it.

It wasn't until the lady was leaving that he found out she was single—since she asked him out.

That was also when he got reminded of Lisa's temper.

Gray had only smiled and thanked the woman, ready to make his excuses, when Lisa said, "Honey, did you want to grill tonight?" And she'd pulled him down to kiss him. On the mouth. *Deliberately* for the lady…who left with an apologetic smile, carrying her dog.

Yup, Lisa had a temper, as he'd witnessed when that yahoo had thrown the kid in the lake. Gray would never forget seeing the guy shout back at her and how he'd wanted to take the man apart.

But in most cases Lisa had great control and even better tact. Overall the customers, visitors and locals alike, loved her.

Some of the hopefuls that Amber had originally brought around still tried to flirt, but she was never more than casually friendly. He respected that a lot.

Lisa didn't need compliments to continually feed her ego. She was smart, talented and accomplished. She knew it but didn't brag about it.

Every damn day he wondered if she could possibly be content in Buckhorn. She didn't seem bored. But neither did she say the menial work fulfilled her.

Shelby loved her. If she didn't stick around, the dog would miss her horribly. In fact, Shelby fretted every morning when Lisa insisted on driving home to jog—for appearances.

Gray didn't tell her that she'd seriously underestimated the intelligence of her family if she thought they hadn't yet figured it out. From what he could tell, they were all observant enough to understand the way of things. Hell, Gray didn't want to hide it.

But apparently Lisa did. So every morning she drove home and jogged and then came back to work with him wearing fresh clothes.

If he had his way he'd just move her in, but her house was nice enough that he supposed that didn't make sense to her.

On the morning of the picnic, as Lisa was preparing to go, Gray walked Shelby downstairs to let her out in the back lot where she usually did her business. She still navigated the stairs with no problem, but at ten, how much longer could that last? Something to think about.

The stairs opened into the shop, and Gray immediately sensed something was wrong. Setting aside his coffee cup, he looked around but saw nothing amiss. Shelby, picking up on his tension or maybe sensing something he didn't, gave a low snarl and crept toward the door that would lead to the back lot.

The dog was normally so passive that the feral sound surprised Gray.

"Easy." He put a hand in her collar in case he needed to restrain her, then opened the door—and stepped into one hell of a mess.

Shelby tried to dart out, but he stopped her. Until he made sure the vandal was gone, he wouldn't take any chances. Turning, he called toward the stairs, "Lisa? I need you."

LISA STOOD BACK with Shelby on her leash, distraught over the destruction done to the lot. Shelby wasn't happy, either, so on top of taking it all in, Lisa did her best to soothe the dog.

Splattered paint covered everything, thrown on the trees and Shelby's new fence and the grass. Vile words covered the back of the building and the trailer for Gray's boat.

His boat.

Oh, no. Pivoting around, urging Shelby to follow, Lisa started down to the docks.

Gray materialized in front of her. He looked scruffy,

intense and all alpha-male protective. "Where are you going?"

Lisa had a hard time answering. Gray hadn't yet put on a shirt or shoes, and his shorts hung low. She knew he tried to keep his expression neutral. Did he fear showing her the anger he surely had to feel?

How had he even noticed her leaving? One moment he'd been talking with Tucker and Morgan, who'd again shown up together. They'd been calculating the damage, going over everything, and then poof, Gray stood there in front of her.

Lisa shifted her bare feet on the dew-wet grass. The sun was up, already scorching the day, but night on the lake always left everything wet with humidity. It'd take another hour at least to dry out the area. "Your trailer is ruined."

"It can be cleaned off, probably with a power washer."

"It can?"

He scratched his bare chest, swatted away a bee and stared down at her. "Wet as everything is, the paint didn't get a good chance to dry. It'll be fine." He dropped his hands back to his hips and asked again, "Where are you headed?"

She hated to say it aloud, but he waited, his gaze never wavering from hers… She winced. "Your boat."

His face went blank before dark emotion flashed into his stormy eyes. "Shit." He took off at a fast clip down to the shore, striding along the boardwalk and then down the dock and—she heard his muttered curse over whatever he found.

He'd been through so much, but he'd found his place

again here. He liked Buckhorn. Really liked it. *Why was someone tormenting him like this?*

Coming up alongside her, Morgan automatically reached for the leash and took the dog from her. Shelby didn't mind. She panted up at Morgan with near adoration. Her uncle, a big softie when it came to animals, squatted down to give the dog attention.

Shelby sniffed him all over.

"She smells your own pets," Lisa told him. Shelby had an amazing nose. Often she'd smell a dog before customers entered with their pets.

"You're a good girl, aren't you?" Morgan said to Shelby, then he looked up at Lisa. "He's made an enemy."

The sudden switch threw her. "Gray? Don't be silly. Everyone loves him."

His brow went up. "Everyone, huh?"

She froze, but quickly shook it off. "With the security lights and knowing Gray lived upstairs, a person would have to be very ballsy to get close enough to do all this."

"Ballsy, or nuts," Morgan said, standing again. "I'm betting on both."

"That's why you're here?"

He shrugged. "Tucker told me when Gray called. Assuming you'd be here, too, I decided to tag along."

Lisa snorted. Morgan might have retired as the sheriff, but he still involved himself in every situation.

"Know what I'm wondering?"

Feeling a trap, Lisa didn't look at him. But that didn't stop her uncle Morgan. Very little ever did.

"I'm wondering why Gray didn't hear anything. He must have been…preoccupied?"

"Or sleeping," she said with a frown. "Don't most people sleep at night?"

"Yeah." Morgan still watched her too closely. "Unless someone is fresh to a romance. Then there are usually better things to be doing, things that could distract a man."

So now she was a distraction?

The sounds of a truck on the gravel drive saved her from replying. Both she and Morgan turned to see Garrett had arrived. Her cousin, Morgan's son, was a firefighter. He was also friends with Tucker. For those reasons, Lisa supposed he had some interest in any mischief caused in Buckhorn.

Looking around again, she took mental inventory of what would be needed to clean and repair everything.

"So you spent the night, huh?"

Startled by that abrupt statement, her gaze clashed with her uncle's again. Her laugh sounded guilty, as did her exclaimed *"What?"*

Morgan looked at the dog, shook his head as if Shelby would understand and then slung an arm around her. "I know the signs, honey, so don't bother denying it. I'm not judging you. I'm just surprised. I mean, that was fast."

Heat rushed into her face. What would Morgan think if he knew she'd originally hooked up with Gray within hours of meeting him?

"Never known you to move fast before."

"Uncle Morgan—"

"I've never known her to move at all," Garrett said, joining them. "She's usually too involved with her work. But Gray seems all right."

They heard Gray muttering curses mixed with threats as he pulled ruined equipment out of his boat.

"All things considered," Morgan said.

"If he coerces her into staying," Garrett added, "then I like him."

"He's not coercing," her dad said, making Lisa jump. "Told me so himself."

Lisa rounded on him, and saw that he had her uncle Sawyer and Shohn with him.

Shohn said, "Hey, cuz," as if they hadn't already intruded.

She threw up her hands. "This is ridiculous. It was vandalism. Why are you all congregating here?"

Sawyer drew her away from Morgan and in for a hug. "Because you're here."

"That's what I told her," Morgan said.

"And Gray," Shohn added, "has an enemy."

"Told her that, too."

"No one wants you caught up in this," her dad told her.

Damn her fair skin, she blushed from her neck to her hairline, and no wonder, with the majority of her male relatives standing there studying her, knowing her and making some accurate guesses.

As her dad searched her face, his brows shot up. He glanced at Morgan, who shrugged. Then at Garrett, who grinned.

Shohn sighed. "Well, hell. You're already in it knee-deep, aren't you?"

CHAPTER EIGHT

THAT PARTICULAR SUNDAY, the family picnic got moved to the marina. With Lisa's enormous family pitching in, the majority of the mess was gone in no time, the dog's fence had been rebuilt, and half a dozen grills sent delicious scents into the air.

They'd even helped run the marina while he dealt with everything else.

That drove it home for him: in Buckhorn, people helped each other. Gray liked that. A lot. It was so different from the city life he'd been used to, especially as a cop.

Petie, who'd worked as hard as anyone, wiped his hands on a towel and eyed Gray. "You're not going to let this run you off, are you?"

Gray laughed. "I was just thinking how glad I am that I moved here."

That pleased Petie. "Glad to hear it."

"Am I interrupting?" Lisa asked as she joined them.

"As if you could," Petie said. He scratched the graying beard stubble on his throat. "Guess I ought to get up to the store. It's lookin' busy." He went off and Shelby, no longer leashed, followed closely behind him.

Gray looked at Lisa. She looked…somehow distant as she stared after the dog.

Was she worried? Gray tipped her chin toward him. "Shelby is fine."

She bit her lip and stayed quiet.

More than once he'd heard her father and uncles expressing concern for her. Until their vandal was caught, her nearness to him could be dangerous.

Did she realize that, too? If so, it might make what he had to do easier—at least for her. "I'm sorry about all this." He put his arms around her and pulled her in. For most of the day she'd been inundated with family, all of them openly speculating. "You okay?"

Leaning back, she stared at him. "Me? I'm fine. I was worried about you."

What the hell? "I can take care of myself."

She laughed. "As can I."

"What? Take care of me?" He liked that idea.

Very seriously, she said, "If you ever need me, I'd be happy to help. But I meant that I can take care of myself, too."

He brought her in for a kiss. "And if you ever need me, for any reason, I'm here for you. You know that, right?" For him, that would never change, no matter how this all worked out.

Her smile went tender, her gaze searching. "So we can take care of ourselves, but we're each willing to care for the other, too?"

"You know what?" Amber said, interrupting the moment. "That sounds like a relationship to me."

With a theatrical groan, Lisa dropped her forehead to Gray's chest. "Why," she lamented, "does my family keep sneaking up on me today?"

"It only feels sneaky," Adam told her, "when you're hiding secrets."

"I'm not!" Lisa snapped, then tucked her face against Gray again.

Gray wisely stayed out of it.

"You are," Amber insisted, not worried about staying out of anything, apparently. "I just don't know why. I mean, we have eyes, you know. And look at him, Lisa. Most ladies would be bragging."

Gray grinned while stroking Lisa's back. "Thank you."

"You're welcome."

"I think it's because they barely know each other." Adam eyed him. "You really rushed things, didn't you?"

Lisa groaned, so Gray did more stroking along her spine. "She's irresistible. I couldn't help myself."

"Seriously?"

Amber shoved Adam. "Don't be a doofus. Uncle Sawyer met Honey and knew she was the one. And Dad met Mom and even though it took them a little longer to work things out, he knew she was special. And *your* dad," she continued, "met Georgia and flipped."

"Yeah," Adam said with a smile. "You're going off what you've been told, but even though I was young, I can still remember the first time Dad stayed over and made us pancakes."

Lisa shifted a little to see the others, but she stayed close. With a smile in her voice, she said, "He used a turkey baster to make the pancakes into shapes. Mom didn't know what to think of him. I remember her looking so confused."

Gray liked hearing the stories. It shored up his belief that sometimes you just knew when someone was the right one. For him, that someone was Lisa. For her… he just didn't know.

"You know," Amber said to Adam. "I have someone in mind for you, too, so if you—"

"What I want to know," Adam said, cutting her off, "is why all this trouble is following Gray."

Lisa pushed away from Gray to confront her brother. "It's not his fault that some idiot is into the destruction of property."

"Never said it was, but if it's the same idiot who wrote that note and damn near strangled a dog, then it has something to do with him, right?"

"He's being targeted!"

"But maybe by someone who knows him?"

Gray tried to interject, but he couldn't get a word in edgewise as the siblings squabbled back and forth. He looked at Amber, saw her smiling and shook his head.

She edged around Lisa and Adam and nudged him with her shoulder. "Usually Lisa is quiet."

"Ha!" Adam said.

"I am quiet!"

Gray grinned. "She's a delicate flower."

Sucking in air, Lisa rounded on him. "Are you saying I'm not?"

"I'm saying you're beautiful and smart and I enjoy you whether you're being pensive or giving your brother hell."

"Ooh," Amber said. "Not only gorgeous, but smooth."

Lisa narrowed her eyes at Amber, which only made Amber laugh. "Lighten up, cuz. If he's going to stick around—"

"He is," Gray confirmed.

"—then he may as well get used to us, right?"

"Not like any of you are giving him a choice."

"It's fine," Gray said. "Better than fine. I appreciate all the help today."

Looking closed off and distant, Lisa didn't reply.

Gray had no idea why she was so out of sorts. Well, except that someone had crept around the yard wreaking havoc while they slept. That could be unnerving her. But he sensed it was something more than that.

Something personal.

Maybe he should get her alone and find out.

He was about to suggest that when Amber hooked her arm through his. "So, Lisa, you're saying you don't have a claim in this one? Because if he's free, I know a few single ladies who would *love* for me to work my magic."

"No, thanks," Gray said hurriedly.

At the same time, Lisa growled, *"Don't even think it."*

"Yeah," Adam said, his tone dry. "Such a delicate flower."

Gray pulled Lisa back when she reached for her brother. "If you guys would excuse us a moment, I think Shelby needs us."

Since Shelby was sprawled under a big tree some distance away, sleeping soundly, it was an obvious lie.

Gray didn't care. Unfortunately, getting Lisa alone was like walking the gauntlet.

First he had to get past Morgan, Misty, Sawyer and Honey. The men looked at him with suspicion, but the women smiled their encouragement. Morgan's wife even gave him the thumbs-up.

Then they went around Gabe's daughters, who had effectively circled Tucker, not that Tucker seemed to mind all that much. Gabe didn't like it, though, and he was fast closing in on them, pausing only long enough to note Gray leading Lisa toward the house.

"Don't do anything I would do," he said to Gray, then pointed at his daughters. "That goes for you three, too."

The girls laughed, but Tucker held up his hands in a sign of innocence…while wearing a big grin.

Yeah, Gray wasn't buying that any more than Gabe did.

Jordan stood with Garrett and Shohn at one of the grills, and they all three stared as Gray, with his hand at Lisa's back, kept her walking.

"Should we save you some food?" Jordan asked mildly, and it looked like he was asking about a lot more than food.

"A burger each, please," Gray said, putting her father at ease. "We won't be long."

Jordan just nodded, but the two younger men snickered—and got threatened with a grill fork.

Inside the store provided no privacy, either, not with Petie now waiting on customers. Going upstairs to his living area would be too damn obvious, so Gray led Lisa right back out the front door, across the gravel lot and toward the large elm tree where Shelby slept on. She'd deliberately found a quiet spot away from the chaos. There were no benches here, only that one lone tree, a chicken-wire fence overgrown with weeds, and what felt like an army of bugs.

"Where," Lisa asked, "are we going?"

"Not sure yet," Gray told her. "So far the tree looks semiprivate, but with your family I'm never sure who might pop up next."

She groaned.

"I like them," Gray reminded her. He glanced back

and saw a lot of people looking their way, but no one followed. Shelby slept on, so Gray kicked down the weeds in one spot, sat and pulled Lisa into his lap. "Now."

She tucked her face into his neck. "They do this sort of thing a lot."

Gray breathed in the scent of her sun-warmed hair and skin, and his body stirred. Nothing new in that. He pretty much wanted her around the clock. It was taking some time to get used to it and to get it under control. "What's that?"

Throwing out an arm, she indicated her family. "They circle the wagons, show up en masse to help out. They're…pretty wonderful."

"I agree." He nuzzled his way along her throat to her jaw, nudging her face up as he went so he could kiss her. "You think they like me okay?"

"They lo—"

His mouth over hers cut off her reply. As always, her soft lips opened to the touch of his tongue. Her breath hitched. She leaned into him, accepting. Participating.

And even here, with weeds poking him in the ass and a mosquito buzzing in his ear, with Shelby's snores and her family's whispers, he could so easily get lost in loving her.

But she was already shy about her family knowing how involved they were, so Gray forced himself to cool it. With one last stroke of his tongue over hers, he retreated, nibbled on her lips, then put his forehead to hers.

"I'm going to find whoever did this."

"Mmm-hmm." She tried to kiss him again.

"Hey." Gray let her take one quick kiss but didn't let

it get too heated. "If we don't put the brakes on that, I won't be able to rejoin your family."

Sliding her arms around his neck, she hugged him. "You confuse me so much."

"Yeah?" The crook of her shoulder, her neck, smelled so good and felt so soft. "How's that, honey?" He stroked his hand up and down her back. No matter what Lisa wore, she always looked stylish and sexy but this, his shirt, thrown on hastily that morning when he'd called her for help, looked better on her than it ever could on him. She hadn't yet changed, so she also had on running shorts and bare feet, and he loved her. Her sleek runner's legs, her rounded ass, those cushiony breasts pressed to his chest. Her mouth. Her hugs and her sighs. Her strength and her humor, and her dedication to her family. Every inch of her, everything about her.

But he wouldn't manipulate her with words into doing anything that she didn't really want. So he kept his love to himself. "Lisa?" She'd gotten awfully quiet.

"You landed here after some pretty horrific circumstances, but now you just roll with it."

"It?"

"Everything. Anything." She shook her head. "Whatever happens."

Mostly because *she* had happened. With her, it didn't matter what else went wrong, it was still going to feel right.

Except that… Gray knew he couldn't take chances with her. He'd brought her here to find out what was on her mind, but realized he also needed to share what was on his.

"Your poor boat," she whispered and hugged him again as if she thought he might need the comfort.

"Yeah. Sucks. But it can be repaired." He brushed back her hair. "You can't."

"What?" She struggled to get free, but he held on.

"I'm going to get the loon who's targeting me. I swear I am. Tucker is on it, and so is your uncle, and everyone in your family is alert and keeping watch. But I don't feel right about you being here. Not until it's resolved."

She shoved back so hard she got away from him and, landing on her butt, bumped into Shelby. The dog jumped, looked at them both, then huffed and resettled herself.

"Are you all right?"

Eyes locked on his, she whispered, "You're ditching me."

"No! Never that." Gray reached for her but she dodged him. "If I could I'd move you in."

Her jaw loosened, then went tight. "You *could*," she said in a voice too high, then glanced at the crowd of her family and lowered her voice. "I've all but moved in on you anyway."

"Right." Bitterness leaking through, Gray said, "That's why you head home every morning so no one will know you spent the night."

She gasped, scowled and scampered closer to stick her face near his. "I was trying to be *considerate*."

"Considerate?" His own temper kicked in. "How the hell do you figure that?"

"You haven't asked me to stay, so I didn't push it. If my family once knew that we…that I…"

Glaring at her, he leaned in, too. "That we're committed to each other? I can say it even if you can't."

"I can say it!" But she faltered. "If it's true."

"Why the hell would you doubt it?"

"I doubt it because all you've done is explain to me how you're hunky-dory however it goes, if I stay, if I leave, oh, well, Gray will be fine."

He plopped back on his ass. "That's what you think?" God, he would *not* be fine if she ended things.

Her brows shot up. "That's what you've said."

"I was trying not to pressure you."

"Great," she snapped right back. "I'm not pressured."

At that moment, it almost struck him as funny, but he didn't dare laugh. Not with Lisa looking both hurt and mad. "I'm in love with you."

Her eyes went wide. *"What?"*

A whisper, not a shout. He smiled. "I love you. Hell, I've been in love with you since I saw you here again. Maybe even before that. Everything about you suits everything in me. I want you with me. I want you here in Buckhorn. But more than that, I want you happy. If your old job does it for you, then I'll—"

She landed against him, kissing his face, tumbling him backward onto the gravel-rough, weed-strewn, root-mangled ground. "Ow," he said and held her close.

"Oh, Gray," she breathed. "Crazy how it happened so fast, but you just said it so beautifully."

"What'd I say?" He couldn't think with her stretched out over him, her heart beating in time with his, a damned audience no doubt watching every move they made.

"Everything about you suits everything in me."

"Oh, right. That."

She laughed. "No, I was saying it to you."

Forgetting the audience, Gray grabbed her shoulders and lifted her. "You love me?"

Her beautiful, devastatingly dark eyes answered

before she said, "Of course I do. You heard Amber." Her lips curled and she added with sassiness, "You're a catch."

He crushed her close, one hand in her hair, an arm across her back. His heart felt…explosive. As if it might punch right out of his chest. "I want you happy," he said again with conviction. He wanted that more than anything.

"I am."

Wanting to believe her, he asked, "Your career…?"

"I don't know, Gray." She kissed his throat, his chin, then nipped his bottom lip. "Somehow I'll work it out. But I don't want to give up you, *this*, just to chase a career I'm not sure I even want."

He searched her face and believed her. She wanted to stay. *With him.* As she'd said, they'd work out everything else. And thinking that, he sat up but kept her on his lap. "We need to talk."

"Gray," she warned.

"I have to know you're safe until I resolve the threat."

"A vandal isn't a threat."

"A vandal who leaves cowardly notes and abuses a stray dog is."

Her small hand settled against his jaw. "I'm not leaving you." She turned her head toward her gathered family members and said louder, "I don't care who knows about it."

Gray was more than ready to insist when Shelby came awake with a start, bolting to her feet, ears up, eyes alert.

Sniffing the air.

"What in the world?" Lisa said, already moving off his lap.

"Hey, girl." Gray stood and reached for the dog, but she stared off toward the weeds along the fence. Her lips curled in a snarl and, hunkering down, she began creeping forward.

Gray stared at the high weeds along the fence. "A critter, maybe?"

Shaken, Lisa shook her head. "I don't think so."

Suddenly Shelby lunged, filling the area with enraged barking as she ran. She went through a hole in the fence and Gray, running after her, went over the fence. He landed in prickly bushes and felt a scratch on his back, another on his leg. Behind him he heard Lisa yell and then the commotion as others followed.

Shelby launched herself and landed on a man holding a gas can. The can nearly dropped out of his hand, spilling everywhere as he attempted to protect himself.

In a matter of seconds Gray took it all in, and comprehension dawned. What looked like a very crude, makeshift bomb had been jammed up against the fence between a dead tree and a metal barrel full of debris, surrounded by dry brush. An oily path led to the man… and the spilled gas can.

The son of a bitch had planned a very big, loud fire.

Dangerous. Especially with so many people at the marina.

Enraged, Gray reached them, took Shelby's collar and hauled her back from the man's flailing fists and legs. Meaning it, he said, "Kick my dog, and I swear to God you'll regret it."

The man scampered back, breathing hard, his eyes a little wild. "Your dog attacked me!"

"Yeah." He kept his eyes on the man, but said, "Good dog."

Luckily, Shelby subsided, sitting down but still tense.

"Easy now." He stared down at the man—the same man who had thrown a kid in a lake, who had argued with Lisa and then been left ashore when his date took off with her son in the boat. Likely the same man who had tied that damned rope too tight around Shelby's neck. "I remember you."

The man kicked out at him, inciting Shelby all over again.

And then suddenly Morgan was there, saying, "Jordan's keeping Lisa back, and I've got the dog for you."

Satisfaction brought a smile to Gray's mouth. He didn't look back to confirm what Morgan said. He trusted him.

Releasing Shelby, he reached for the man.

Panicked, the idiot swung the gas can in an awkward arc. Gray ducked—and then drilled him. One clean shot to the chin that took the guy's feet out from under him. He went flat again, the can falling well out of his reach.

Suddenly Tucker snapped, "What the hell? Damn you, Morgan, why didn't you tell me?"

"You were busy flirting with Kady. Besides, I wanted to let Gray hit him a few times first."

Gray took advantage of that confession, hauling the man up and punching him one more time before Tucker bellowed, "That's enough!"

Knowing the procedure, Gray stepped back and began explaining everything while Tucker put the man in handcuffs.

Lisa joined him then, half her family following along. She stopped by Shelby, kneeling down to hug the dog. Shelby glanced at her, licked her face, then stared with evil intent at the man being led away.

Shohn and Garrett had just walked the fence. "The gas is all along the base of the fence," Shohn said. "Guess he planned a big fire."

"Guaranteeing he'd get away," Garrett said.

Still furious, Gray nodded. "It'd be hard to pursue him if we had to go through flames to do it."

Garrett surveyed everything, then rubbed the back of his neck. "I'm thinking you'll have to close the marina for a day so we can burn it off. Better that we do it before some kid gets more than he bargained for playing with matches."

"Agreed." Gray stared at Lisa. She hadn't yet come to him. "Lisa?"

She stayed by Shelby but looked up at him. With her cousins and uncles around her and other family crowding in, she said, "So I don't have to go back to my house."

Damn, but he loved her. He didn't look at anyone else, never broke eye contact with her. He just smiled. "No, you don't."

"This is one of those times," Morgan said, "when *not* being the cop is a good thing. Tucker will be tied up for hours with that ass, and you're free and clear."

"Yeah." Gray went to Lisa, pulled her up and against him and then kissed her silly.

He vaguely heard her brother say, "I feel like I should be protesting this."

"Do," Amber said, "and she'll annihilate you."

It wasn't until Shelby leaned against his leg that he managed to end the kiss. With one hand on Shelby's neck, the other at Lisa's waist, he said, "I love you."

She nodded, smiled. Blinked back a few tears. "I love you, too."

There was more murmuring about *fast*, but Gray ignored them all.

Shohn spoke up. "Does this mean you're staying?"

Gray was about to tell him not to pressure her, but Lisa said, "Yes!"

And then her family did so much cheering and carrying on that he couldn't get anything said. Men were shaking his hand, women were hugging him. He got separated from Lisa while the congrats went around.

He'd just gotten to her when Amber threw herself against him, squeezing him tight. For a slight woman, she had her fair share of strength.

Laughing, Gray accepted the hug until she dropped back to her feet. The second she freed him, he pulled Lisa close again.

"We're alone," Amber said to the two of them, "so I have a couple of things to say to you."

Lisa leaned into his side. "Beware, Gray. She has that intense look in her eyes that means she's about to shock us."

Amber started to speak but pulled back. "Do I really? I mean, I've heard that before. That I give myself away." Hands on her hips, more to herself than anyone else, she muttered, "Maybe that's why I can't catch Noel off guard."

"Noel?" Gray asked.

"Noel Poet," Lisa explained. "He's a firefighter with Garrett, and Amber's boyfriend."

Amber snorted. "He's never even kissed me, so how could he be my boyfriend?"

"My guess?" Gray smiled at her. "You probably scare the poor guy."

Amber looked thoughtful for a moment, then dismissed that notion with a shake of her head. "I don't scare you, right?"

"No." Because he'd only have peripheral involvement with her, through Lisa. But if he'd ever thought to get close to her, then hell, yes, she would scare him.

"There. I'm not scary at all."

"If I could make a suggestion?" Gray waited until he had the attention of both women. "If you want to kiss him, make a move. No reason you should have to wait."

"Hmm. You know, you could be right. If he was here today instead of on duty, I'd give it a shot just to see his reaction."

Gray grinned. Yeah, he believed her. Amber Hudson wouldn't shy away from many things—definitely not a man.

She shook her head. "So anyway, back to you guys. I was waiting, holding back until—"

He and Lisa both laughed.

"—I knew for sure you'd be working it out." She winked at Gray. "You haven't disappointed me. I don't even think you needed the incentive of the other guys I brought around to get you motivated."

Gray wasn't surprised to learn that had been her ploy. "When it comes to Lisa, believe me, I'm very self-motivated."

"So I see."

"Amber," Lisa warned.

Amber leaned to look beyond them, around them, then she said, "High five, cuz."

Confused but compliant, Lisa smacked palms with Amber.

"Sometimes," Amber told her, "a one-night stand

turns into forever. I'm proud of you! You went for it, so kudos to you."

Lisa went mute and Gray frowned. "How…?"

Waving a hand, Amber explained, "I knew where Lisa had traveled, and after grilling Gray when I first met him, I knew where he'd been. The timing lined up, so it seemed obvious to me, especially after seeing the two of you together. But don't worry. Your secret is safe with me."

Gray rubbed his face. Yeah, she was scary, all right.

"Now, about you staying in Buckhorn." Amber smiled at her red-faced cousin. "Have you thought about working remotely? Casey does it sometimes and he said all you'd really need is reliable internet, a quiet place to work, some meeting software and *voilà!* Cybermeetings, instead of face-to-face, are the in thing. You work out all the deets in online meetings, then limit your travel to a few days a month. What do you think?"

After a few expectant seconds when Lisa looked thunderstruck, she grabbed Amber, squealing as she hugged her.

Amber laughed with her. "So you like the idea?"

"I love the idea!" Lisa gave her cousin a big smooch, then held her away. "I can't believe I didn't think of it. I mean, I've been involved in cybermeetings for different clients. I've just been so stressed, and then Gray was here, and…" Winding down, she said, "You're a genius."

"That's what I keep telling people." She held up her hand and Gray high-fived her as well. "My work here is done. Oh, how I love a happy ending." Clearly pleased with herself, Amber moseyed off.

Gray brought Lisa around for a quick kiss. "You think that would actually work?"

"As Amber said, it's the in thing. My company wants me, so I think they'll be all over it."

He searched her face and had to ask, "It'll make you happy?"

"You make me happy. Shelby makes me happy." She inched closer. "Keeping my job but losing all the travel will make me happy."

He grinned. "Then I'm happy, too." He touched her face. "And since you're compromising, what do you think about me doing the same?"

"How?"

"I'm not rushing you, I promise. But I want to marry you, and when we do—"

"Gray." She threw herself against him, bounced a little, then grabbed his face and kissed him.

Gray didn't mind the interruption, not with Lisa holding him tight, bubbling with excitement. But as the kiss ended, he grinned and asked, "Is that a yes?"

"Yes!"

Happiness threatened to take out his knees, but he stiffened his legs and kept her close to his heart. "We won't need two houses. Doesn't matter to me where we live, so either I'll rent out my house and Shelby and I will live with you, or you can sell your place and live here with us. I know it's small, but I thought it was just going to be me. Now that it's us, you and me and Shelby, we can remodel or add on."

She covered her mouth.

Gray hurried to say, "Or we can keep both and worry about it later. Or buy something new. Or build, or—"

"Gray." She said his name this time with tears in her

eyes and a trembling smile. "Yes to marrying you, yes to having only one house for you and me and Shelby, but I honestly don't care which one." She inhaled, brushed a tear from her cheek. "Yes to loving you."

"And yes to staying in Buckhorn?"

"It's my home," she whispered. "I've always enjoyed it, but now that you're here, I never want to leave."

Together, they turned to head back to the gathering of her family. Lisa spotted Amber saying something to Adam while Adam tried to shake his head and refuse.

Lisa grinned. "It looks like my brother might be next on Amber's radar."

"Good. He's a nice guy. He should be happy." When Lisa slanted a dubious look up at him, Gray said, "What? She does good work. I trust she'll do right by him."

Lisa laughed over that, but she didn't deny it. Amber had been helpful, not that either of them had really needed a nudge.

Mingling into the crowd of Lisa's big family, with her at his side, Gray recognized the truth. He'd left behind his old life and all the strife. He'd have been happy with the slower lifestyle, the change of pace.

Instead, he'd gotten so much more.

Because now, he had it all.

* * * * *

BACK TO BUCKHORN

I never know where a story (or characters) might take me, so I like to have info up front. Now, though, I feel like I have enough great research material to write many more firefighters! To all the following people who answered firefighter questions, thank you very, very much!

Katie Fairbanks, Deborah Lamoree, Andrew Naylor, Walter Fairbanks, Brian Wood, Joan Swan & Rick. You all rock!

CHAPTER ONE

SUNGLASSES SHIELDING HIS eyes from the hot afternoon sun, Garrett Hudson watched the front of the airport, scanning each female who strode out. He could have gone inside to baggage claim, but then he might've missed her. He stayed on the alert; people changed over time, and there was a good chance Zoey would look right past him. Though she'd had a few brief visits back to the area, they hadn't seen each other in years, and she expected his sister, Amber, to be her ride. But a busted pipe at the bookstore had sidelined Amber, and he got recruited at the last minute, which meant he was running late.

Would he recognize her? How much had she changed? He remembered her as the quirky girl from high school, the one who had danced without caring what others thought, who laughed at the oddest things.

Often the odd girl out, not that she'd ever seemed to care.

He remembered her being kind, always speaking up for the underdog, always befriending the other odd ducks, not because she minded going it alone, but because she knew they did.

What he remembered most about her, though, was her mouth. Full lips. Soft smiles. An easy laugh.

Not only did she have the sexiest mouth he'd ever seen, but she also talked a lot. Sometimes nonstop.

Back then, he'd been amused by her.

And he'd always wanted to kiss her. Badly.

For the tenth time, he checked his watch. When he looked up again, a new crowd of people surged out, dragging luggage along in their wake. He scanned each face, his gaze going past an older couple, a young mother with a kid, a bedraggled brunette—

His attention zipped back.

No way. Could it be? He'd think not, except for the way she zeroed in on him while biting her lip. That was a tip-off.

Zoey had always bit her lip when uneasy.

Damn. What the hell had happened to her?

She looked… Trying to be kind, he decided on *not good.*

Starting forward, he called out, "Zoey Hodge?"

She stared right at him, proving she did, in fact, recognize him. That probably accounted for the lip biting, too. He knew he'd always made her nervous…which was why he'd never gotten that kiss.

Anytime he'd made a move, she'd dodged him.

When he got close, she groaned and covered her face with both hands. And stood there. On the walkway in front of the airport with people forced to move around her.

"Zoey?" Pushing his sunglasses to the top of his head, Garrett bent to see her face. She stood several inches shorter than his six-two. Given the clothes she wore, he had no idea about her build.

But she smelled like throw-up. "Zoey." Why wouldn't she look at him?

"Can you just go away?"

He straightened. "Come again?"

She made a shooing motion with one small hand, then quickly covered her face again. "I'll get a bus. Or cab. Or…I'll walk if I need to."

Hands on his hips, Garrett considered her, but because he needed to be back at work soon, he decided to just take charge. In most instances, with most people, that worked.

He scooped up one bag, grabbed the handle of the other. "I'm taking your luggage." He stepped away…and waited.

Dropping her hands with an overly dramatic sigh, she said, "Fine! Suffer me."

Her makeup was everywhere, making her green eyes a focal point in her face, which was framed by badly tangled, dark brown hair.

But that mouth…damn, it looked as good as ever.

Ignoring her comment—what could he say?—he started off. "I'm parked this way." She grudgingly followed.

Trailing behind him, she said, "I don't always look like this."

God, he hoped not. "Want to tell me what happened?"

As if she'd been waiting for him to ask, she started babbling. "There was a crying kid on the plane. He puked on me. I'd checked all of my luggage instead of carrying it on, so the mother gave me this—" she looked down at the baggy gray T-shirt "—this *thing* to wear. I think it was her husband's. Anyway, I got most of the mess washed off my face and chest, but there wasn't enough water in the tiny bathroom to get it out of my hair. I smell bad. I look bad." She pointed at him. "And *you* had to show up?"

His mouth quirked. Yeah, he'd always remembered Zoey Hodge as being different. Eccentric.

Original.

Off the top of his head, he couldn't remember any other woman screeching at him in accusation. "What's wrong with me?"

Her expression said it should have been obvious. "You're *you*."

"Okay." What the hell did that mean?

She bit her lip again. "That is...well, you know I had a crush on you in high school."

"You did?" News to him. Hell, *he'd* had a crush, but had never acted on it.

"Well, of course I did."

With no idea what to say, he just nodded.

"And," she continued with emphasis, "when you see an old crush after so many years, well, it'd be better not to reek, right?"

"You're fine," he lied. The baking sun amplified the smell, so he was glad when they finally got into the covered garage.

"I was all set to explain to Amber, to maybe even laugh about it—"

"Really?" He couldn't imagine.

"—and instead *you're* here, seeing me like this, making me even more humiliated and—"

"Amber had a small catastrophe. I was the only one available."

"Catastrophe?" She stopped dead in her tracks. "Is she all right?"

"She's fine. Her bookstore's a little soggy, though, thanks to a broken pipe."

She started walking at a fast clip to catch up with him. "Oh, man." She pushed back her long matted hair. "Well…I don't mean to be ungrateful."

"You're out of sorts." Under the circumstances, she had a right to be grouchy, but she wasn't. More like frazzled, and plenty embarrassed.

They reached his truck and he put the bags in the back then went around to open her door for her. "We can leave the windows down and the smell won't be so bad." He hoped.

She groaned dramatically and got in. Poor thing. She even had stains on the top of her sneakers.

She noticed him looking and wrinkled her nose. "It's in my shoes. I can feel it squishing when I walk."

Sympathy kept the smile off his face.

One hand on the roof, the other on the door frame, Garrett watched her buckle up. Out of the blinding sunlight, he saw that no part of her had been spared. Her hair. Her face. Her jeans. Only the god-awful, too-big, men's gray shirt was clean, but it didn't add much to the getup. "The kid really hurled on you, huh?"

She turned to him, shading her eyes against the sun. "The little guy was so sick."

Even under the unusual circumstances, something about her had him analyzing all her features. Big green eyes, slightly upturned nose and that lush mouth. She had small hands and delicate wrists, so she was probably still slight of build. But under the clothes, Garrett couldn't tell for sure.

Yeah…and he should probably quit trying to tell. Forcing his gaze up to her face, he said, "That's rough."

Nodding, she said, "My heart just broke for him. Two years old and miserable on that plane. And his poor exhausted parents, they were doing everything they could. When he got distracted with me, I thought, well, good. Right?"

She didn't give him a chance to answer.

"Finally he wasn't crying. And I like kids, enough that I didn't mind entertaining him."

He remembered her as always being kind. Most people stuck on a plane with a noisy kid would gripe about it. Not Zoey. She'd tried to help. Nice.

"He was in my lap when he started retching." She wrinkled her nose. "Ever seen a kid projectile-vomit?"

"Uh, no." Thank God.

"I tried to…catch it." She held out a cupped hand to show what she meant.

The smile broke. "Yeah? How'd that work out?"

"It was like a shower of puke." She scrunched her face up more. "Who knew such a small kid could hold so much?"

Laughing, Garrett closed the door and walked around. As soon as he got behind the wheel, she continued.

"I didn't really think about it. It was like…reflex or something, ya know?"

"Sure."

"As a firefighter, maybe you'd have known how to handle it better."

He gave her a disbelieving stare—and her mouth twitched.

"That was reaching, right?" Humor made her eyes even brighter, a beautiful focal point of color in her face.

"But firefighters are heroic and all that so I'm sure you'd have figured out something."

Definitely not his area of expertise. "Let's hope I'm never put to the test."

"He kept twisting around," she said, still trying to explain how she'd gotten covered, "and I was trying to keep him from spraying anyone else—and that's when he got me head-on." Leaning toward him, she whispered, "It filled my bra."

His gaze dipped to her chest again, but being covered in puke took the fun out of boobs, so he only made a noncommittal sound, then started the truck and backed out of the cramped parking space. "You seem like a natural. Do you work with kids for a living?"

"No. I work—*worked*—for a pet groomer. Now I hope to set up my own shop here."

"Planning to stay?"

She waffled...and then changed the subject. "Amber already told me that you're a firefighter. Do you like it?"

He nodded. "We're a small department. A mix of hired and volunteer guys."

"I'd love to see the station sometime."

"Sure."

"Do you do all that PR stuff, like visiting the school and teaching fire safety classes and reminding people about their smoke detectors?"

"We do." He enjoyed interacting with his community, always had. "I like visiting the school the most." He slanted her a look. "That is, as long as no one is chucking."

She laughed—and damn it, he liked it. Her laugh could make him forget about the smell of toddler throw-up.

When he went to exit the airport lot, she scrambled for her purse. "I've got it."

"No worries." He had the ticket and bills already handy, and reached out the window to give both to the woman staffing the payment booth.

The woman peered in the car, gave Zoey an odd look and lifted the gate for them to leave.

Groaning, Zoey sat stiff and straight in the seat. "What must she think?"

"You'll never see her again. Don't worry about it."

"This is awful." She held out her shirt, touched her hair. "I'm trying not to get your truck too messy."

"It'll wash."

"I'll pay you to have it done. And for the parking fee, too."

"Zoey?"

She bit her lip again. "Hmm?"

"It's not a big deal."

"Ha!" Her eyes widened over her own telling reaction.

"So it is a big deal?" Because she'd had a crush on him? Or maybe because she was still interested?

"No. Not at all."

He wasn't buying it. "Just take a breath and relax."

In a rush, she launched into more conversation. "So are your kids just incredibly healthy or do you not have any?"

"No kids." He steered onto the highway and headed home.

"Married?"

"Nope." He glanced her way, but didn't see a ring on her finger. "You?"

"God, no."

Such a heartfelt denial made him frown. Seven years ago, after she broke things off with her boyfriend, Gus Donahue, Gus had left in a rage.

Then crashed his car and died, leaving his parents with two children instead of three, robbing them of their firstborn.

For too many people, she'd been the undeserving girl, while Gus had been the all-star golden boy. He'd been viewed as perfect.

She was not.

The blame and accusations had rolled in, spurred on by the Donahues, unrelentingly cruel until, finally, she'd moved away to escape it.

Never had Garrett blamed her, but even long after Zoey had left, Gus's sister, Carrie, had done what she could to keep fueling the fire. And Cody, forever feeding the stories, had grown into a very angry sixteen-year-old, always acting out, probably doing what he could to overcome the distance of his parents' grief.

Garrett didn't want to get into all that old history with her. What kind of welcome would that be? Instead he asked, "Any serious relationships?"

She shook her head. "I take it you and Carrie didn't make it?"

Gently, assuming it had to still be a touchy topic for her, he said, "That was...what? Six years ago? Seven?"

Her expression turned quizzical. "Since I left, yes. That's when you and Carrie broke up?"

"Shortly thereafter." He couldn't abide the way Carrie and her family reviled Zoey. They'd taken every opportunity to run her into the ground. He'd understood their grief, and he'd also understood what a hothead Gus had been.

Most of all he'd understood that the Donahues had two children left who needed their attention.

"And here everyone thought you two were the 'it' couple."

"Not me." Carrie was as popular as her older brother, and that, more than anything else, had prompted him to date her.

Yeah, he'd been young and foolish, ruled more by testosterone than discretion.

Looking out the window, Zoey changed the topic. "I need to shower and change before I see anyone."

He was supposed to drop her off at the bookstore, but he could afford the time for a quick detour. "Where to then?"

"I don't know." She looked back at him. "My mom's in the hospital."

"I heard." Everyone knew everyone's business in Buckhorn, at least to some degree. "How is she?"

"She fell off her horse, broke her hip and a few ribs."

"Ouch." He winced in sympathy.

"The breaks are bad enough, but now she has pneumonia on top of it."

"The immobility probably helped that along." Garrett knew her mother had had Zoey later in life. Knowing Zoey to be around twenty-four or—five, her mom would be in her mid-sixties. "She'll be okay?"

"Yes," she said with absolute conviction, as if she could will it so. "But I'm not sure yet when she'll get to come home. They already did the surgery on her hip, but she'll go to a different floor for rehab before they release her." She repeatedly pleated and smoothed the hem of her shirt.

"Is that where you want me to take you?"

She shook her head hard. "No, not looking like this. I don't want to embarrass her." Her fingers curled into a fist. "She's been living with my uncle the last few years, but there's no way I can go there, either."

Her uncle had been the football coach when Gus died. Shit.

"I don't suppose you'd loan me your shower?"

Garrett shot her a look, but she didn't seem to think a thing of her request. Typical of Zoey. Trying not to be too obvious, he checked the clock on the console. "If we make it quick, I have enough time."

Relief took the tension out of her shoulders. "Thank you. I promise to be as fast as I can."

"No problem." But damn it, when he saw Amber, he'd let her know that her debt to him had just doubled.

NEVER HAD SHE met a man so hard to read.

Garrett Hudson, with his dark hair and incendiary blue eyes, didn't seem to react to anything. He'd seen her standing there in her vomit-covered clothes, smelling of it, and he hadn't blinked an eye.

He had to put her in his truck, and he just rolled with it. No fuss, no big deal. No censure or disdain.

Zoey should have remembered his even temper and iron control, but she hadn't been expecting him.

No, she'd been looking for Amber—and when she'd spied Garrett instead, she'd whispered a quick prayer that he would look past her so she could slink away.

She never had been the lucky sort.

Even though he hadn't let the appearance or smell get to him, he was her fantasy guy, her biggest regret, and he'd just found her looking as bad as any woman could.

Worse, she had to impose on him to use his shower.

But good God, it was bad enough that he had to see her like this. She didn't want to face the rest of the town looking like she'd been regurgitated from an ailing giant.

Zoey was pretty sure things couldn't get any worse… until Garrett pulled up to an older Cape Cod and she saw two of his cousins in his driveway. It was all she could do to keep from groaning in agony.

Shohn Hudson was a year older, Adam Sommerville four years older, and they were both amazing specimens.

She tried to sink lower in the seat while Garrett quickly put the truck in Park and got out. "What's going on?"

Shohn said, "Not much. Just had a few quick questions for you. Since Adam and I were heading out to dinner, we just stopped by."

Hiding inside the truck, Zoey looked over the men. Amber had caught her up on all the family dynamics, so she knew Shohn, now engaged, was a park ranger. Seeing him in his uniform, his hair dark, his eyes darker, she'd be willing to bet a lot of women chose to get lost in the woods.

As a gym teacher, Adam stayed in amazing shape. A growing breeze teased his messy blond hair, and when he took off his sunglasses to see into the truck, she got stuck staring into sincere, chocolate-brown eyes.

Smile going crooked, Zoey waved.

"Who do you have in there?" Adam asked with a confused frown.

Only then did Shohn even notice her. He peered into the truck, too, and Zoey knew she had to quit being a coward.

Straightening the ugly gray T-shirt, she opened the door and got out.

Hands on his hips, head dropped forward, she knew Garrett resigned himself to explaining her unwelcome presence.

Nervousness always made her babble. "Hi. I'm Zoey Hodge." Gray clouds rolled in, which she appreciated. The bright sunlight only ramped up the smell and showed all the mess more clearly. "Hey, Shohn. We weren't in the same grade, but I knew you from school." She watched for signs of recognition, but he only stared at her. "No? Well, that's okay. I didn't really expect you to remember."

Shohn looked her over with doubt, and stayed quiet.

"But Adam, you're older, right? I mean, of course I remember you. Duh. All the girls knew you. But I doubt you ever noticed me."

Adam got his faculties working first and reached out to greet her. "Hi. Nice to—"

"No!" She held up a hand. "I got puked on."

Adam froze, then, as one, the two men turned to stare at Garrett.

He let out a breath. "On the plane. Sick kid she helped care for." He gestured. "Amber asked me to pick her up since she was dealing with that busted pipe."

They turned to look at Zoey again.

"Garrett's going to let me use his shower."

Eyes widening, their gazes shot right back to their cousin.

Flustered, especially at how she'd blurted that, Zoey continued, "He's been supernice, especially considering..." She gestured at herself. Unfortunately, the men were all downwind of her. It'd be best if she wrapped this up. "And Garrett, seriously, I appreciate it so much. I don't know how I can thank you enough."

"Not a big deal."

"Of course it is." Anxious to escape, she inched toward the back of his truck. "How about I take you to dinner sometime? It's the least I could do, right?"

Garrett shook his head. "No, that's not necessary."

"I insist." She bit her lip, saw that all three men noticed and quickly forced a smile. "I'll just…" Turning, she strode to the truck bed to get her luggage.

"I'll get it," Garrett said.

"It's okay." The last thing she wanted to do was be more of a nuisance. She lifted the heaviest suitcase over the side of the truck bed. "I have it—" But in her haste, she lost her hold and the suitcase hit the ground.

Then popped open.

A bra and a two pair of underwear fell out.

She snatched up the bra and one skimpy pair of panties with lightning speed, sticking both under the rest of the clothes.

She was reaching for the other pair of panties when a big breeze rolled them over the driveway and up against Garrett's shoes.

"Ground," she said with soft desperation, "swallow me whole, please."

Brows raised, Garrett picked up the sheer beige lacy scrap meant to dredge up pure male fantasies.

After grabbing the closest top and shorts, she slammed the case closed and hurried to Garrett. Holding out a hand, hoping to brazen her way through the uncomfortable moment, she said, "Thank you."

Looking more than a little stymied, he handed the underwear to her.

"Shower?" she prompted, hoping to get things going.

"Sure." He cleared his throat. To his cousins, he said, "You guys want to come in?"

They started making quick excuses, as if they thought he was entertaining her. She shook her head. They surely knew better but probably hoped to put him on the spot for fun. She remembered well how they all liked to tease each other.

"I'm just showering," she explained with a wrinkled nose. "That's all. No hanky-panky. I mean…look at me."

Shohn cocked a brow.

Adam tried to check his amusement, but she saw his smile.

"No, don't look at me," she corrected. Good God, the last thing she wanted right now was a closer scrutiny. "Look at *him*." She pointed at Garrett. "Clearly you guys know he and I aren't…well, you know. Right?"

Garrett was as gorgeous now as he'd been when she'd left. Possibly more so. Out here in the bright sunshine, his black hair glinted with blue highlights. And his eyes… She sighed. Sinfully gorgeous, as light as a summer sky but twice as wicked, with those incredibly long, dark lashes…

When she realized she was staring at him, and everyone else was staring at her, she demanded, "Make your cousins come in."

"You heard her." Garrett gestured. "A storm's rolling in. It'll be best if she finishes up before that."

"I'll hurry," she promised again.

As he unlocked the front door, Garrett said, "Soon as I get you settled, I'll move your luggage into the cab behind the seat in case the rain starts."

"Thank you."

With Adam and Shohn staying several feet behind her—probably to avoid breathing her in—they stepped inside the house.

Zoey stopped and stared. "Holy cow."

For the first time since they'd arrived at his place, Garrett seemed to relax. "Like it?"

Head back, she looked around at the cove ceilings, then down at the high baseboards. "It's incredible." Everything looked vintage, but also shiny and new.

He checked his watch, then said, "If you finish in enough time, I'll show you around."

Oh, shoot. She was holding him up again. "Lead the way."

As he headed for the stairs, they passed a cozy living room on the left, an impressive study on the right. Straight ahead she could see a beautiful country kitchen. Everything looked quaint and original, but in really good shape.

At the top of the stairs, immediately to her right, was the bathroom. Stopping at a closet he got out two big, fluffy white towels, a washcloth and a blow-dryer. "Shampoo, soap and all that is already in the shower." In the all-white bathroom, he lowered the toilet lid and set everything on top of it.

She could have guessed he'd be a neat freak. Men as controlled and contained as him wouldn't appreciate clutter.

Unfortunately, she was a messy, cluttered catastrophe.

"So much character."

He did a double take.

"The house, I mean."

He studied her as if he'd never seen a woman before.

"I've always thought so." He looked around. "There's just something about an older building and all the extra detail put into it."

She nodded. The freestanding tub had a shower stand at one end, an oval curtain rod suspended from the ceiling. "It's just…awesome."

"Pipes are old. Might take a minute for the water to get hot."

"I bought an older house too, but judging by the pictures I've seen, it's nothing like this."

"Pictures?"

"Your sister helped me pick it out."

"You bought it without seeing it?"

She shrugged. "Yeah. I needed a place." For herself—and her mother. Her house would need a year of work before she even got close to this perfection. "Maybe I can show it to you sometime."

Appearing curious, he said, "Sure."

Forgetting herself, Zoey put the clothes—panties on top—with the towels. The glossy subway tiles on the wall drew her fingertips. "This looks vintage, but can't be. It's in such great shape."

"I redid most of it using the same style. Salvaged what I could, but yeah, a lot is new."

Maybe she'd be able to get some pointers from him. About to ask him, she glanced his way and found him staring at her panties again. Taking one big step she put herself in front of the clothes. "Thanks again. I'll only be a few minutes."

Still he stood there, watching her in a funny way.

"I think I've got it from here."

His gaze went over her face, then he shook his head

and started out. "If you need anything else, let me know."

After moving her luggage, Garrett walked into the kitchen, where he knew Shohn and Adam would be waiting to rib him. The second they saw him, he said, "Shut up."

Shohn laughed. "You gotta admit, it's pretty funny."

"Not from her perspective, I'm sure."

"Yeah, probably not." Shohn asked, "A kid really threw up on her?"

"Yeah." He relayed the story.

"Almost happened to me once," Adam admitted. "A fifth-grade girl came up, said she was sick and started gagging. I got a garbage can under her in the nick of time, and it was still gross. Felt really bad for her, too. The other kids teased her until I made them all run laps."

Garrett wondered how Zoey felt about walking through the airport in such a messy state. Had she gotten stares? Whispers? She'd put up with it in school. She shouldn't have to put up with it still.

"So..." Opening the fridge and searching around, Shohn helped himself to a cola. "Why's she using your shower?"

"Like she said, she just flew in."

"She's not from around here?"

He shook his head. "She moved away back when I was a senior. Remember Gus Donahue?"

"He's that guy who died in a car wreck, right?" Buckhorn rarely lost one of their own, and when they did, especially a kid, they remembered.

Adam frowned with the memory. "Jumped a hill and wrapped his car around a tree."

Distracted, Garrett pulled out a chair. "Upstairs in my shower is Zoey Hodge."

Shohn dropped into a chair across from him. "The girl who broke up with him?"

"The girl," Adam said with a frown, "who too many blamed?"

"One and the same."

The old pipes in the house rattled when the water came on. Both his cousins looked up at the ceiling as if they could see her showering overhead.

They looked with sympathy, but damn, even with the surprise of her wrecked appearance, Garrett was starting to feel a little differently. Maybe because no woman had ever used his shower.

Or maybe because she bit that full bottom lip the same way he'd always imagined doing.

Or it could be those hot little panties she'd soon be slipping into…

"She's moving back?" Shohn asked.

"Here for a visit, far as I know. Her mom got hurt pretty bad when she fell from her horse. Zoey will be helping out. But the mom had been staying with the uncle—"

"Who was Gus's coach." Adam let out a low whistle. "Surely he doesn't blame her?"

"No way," Shohn said. "Not after all this time."

Garrett shrugged at them both. "Don't know." But he remembered Coach Marchum being a real asshole. "She didn't seem interested in going there, though, and I couldn't see taking her straight to the bookstore without letting her clean up first."

The water shut off and they all looked up again. True

to her word, she'd made it quick. And right now, she'd be stepping out.

Naked. Wet.

Knowing he needed to get his thoughts back on safer ground, Garrett turned to Shohn. "What did you need to talk about?"

Sitting back in his seat, his gaze speculative, Shohn sprawled out his legs. "Remember that damned fire at the lake? The one where everyone scattered before you could figure out who'd started it?"

"I do." What had probably started as a group of high schoolers roasting marshmallows and indulging in a little necking, got out of hand when a knucklehead decided to toss in some fireworks. They'd gone off and started a dozen small fires. No real damage, but next time could be different, so it wasn't something they'd entirely overlook. "We're still asking some questions about that, but you know how it is. None of the kids want to be a snitch."

"I was hoping you'd found a name or two because there was another fire like it at the park."

Garrett sat forward…until Shohn waved him back.

"The fire was already cold when I found it, and whoever set it did a good job of keeping it contained. But there were fireworks wrappers left around the area." He shook his head. "Bottle rockets and dry conditions do not mix in the woods."

"And we both know which knucklehead has a tendency to dick around with bottle rockets."

"I'll snoop around," Shohn said with a nod. "See if he was camping out that night."

Just what this situation didn't need. "Shit." Squeezing the bridge of his nose, Garrett fought off a headache.

"Not enough sleep?" Adam asked.

"I'm fine." But yeah, he'd been up most of the night with his shift, then had talked with a few Scout leaders about letting their kids come in for a tour. He still had a dozen things to do today, and—

He froze as he suddenly heard singing. Off-key singing.

They all grinned.

Garrett didn't mean to laugh at her, but wow, she sounded bad, maybe even worse than she'd looked. "She's probably using the blow-dryer and doesn't realize how loud she's being."

"Or," Shohn said, "she doesn't care."

Adam cocked a brow. "You think?"

"If I'm remembering right, she always was a little out there."

"Yeah?"

"A real free spirit," Shohn explained.

Garrett narrowed his eyes. "Thought you didn't remember her?"

"Not with how she looks now, no. But since you jogged my memory, it's coming back to me."

Adam watched him. "You going to take her up on dinner?"

Shohn scoffed at the idea. "No offense, but you saw her. He'll find a way out of it."

But how? Garrett didn't want to hurt her feelings.

When the singing suddenly stopped, he froze. They all listened. Hell, Garrett even held his breath. But she made not a single sound on the stairs.

And then suddenly she was there, striding barefoot down the short hall to the kitchen.

The air left his lungs in a low exhalation.

Without even realizing it, he pushed back his chair and stood.

Shohn and Adam did the same.

They all gawked at her.

Zoey held her dirty clothes wrapped in the gray T-shirt. Freshly washed long brown hair hung in soft waves, pulled over one shoulder to cover her left breast.

Supershort, white-cuffed shorts left her entire long, shapely legs bare, and the peach-colored halter emphasized the shape and swell of modest B-sized breasts.

Her bare shoulders were lightly kissed by the sun, her green eyes bright with amusement, her mouth—*God, that mouth*—curved as she appreciated his reaction.

With a small curtsy, she said, "Better, right?"

They all nodded.

Adam got it together first, at least enough to say, "Incredible."

Zoey laughed.

"Hard to believe," Shohn murmured, "that you're the same woman."

Her small nose wrinkled. "Throw-up has a way of making everything pretty icky." She turned those big green eyes on Garrett. Her teeth sank into that plump bottom lip as she searched his face, then her smile widened. "What do you think?"

He thought he wanted that mouth, in about a dozen different ways. He cleared his throat. "Dinner sounds great. I'm off next Saturday."

CHAPTER TWO

TONIGHT SHE'D GET to take Garrett to dinner.

Zoey smiled, thinking about how nicely her first week back had gone, especially given how she'd dreaded it. She'd expected unfriendly reunions, awkward greetings and ugly stares of condemnation.

Instead, for one reason or another, she'd seen Garrett almost every day. The town was small, so every time she turned around she ran into him.

Each and every time he stopped to talk with her.

Each and every time her infatuation with him grew.

Never mind that he was a big, sexy hunk with an easy smile and a hero's personality. He was…well, everything else, too. Friendly, respectable, admired, liked—not just by her, but apparently everyone else, as well.

A few times she'd seen him at his sister's bookstore when Amber invited her for lunch. Amber didn't close the shop during her visit, but it was a slower time for her and few people stopped in.

Yet somehow, each time, Garrett showed up.

Amber also took her to dinner—at Nadine's house, with Shohn and Adam and some of the other cousins there, again, including Garrett. She loved Nadine's pet hotel, and she really enjoyed seeing Nadine and Shohn interact.

They all had pets, and all swore they'd be giving her plenty of business once she opened her grooming salon.

It seemed to Zoey that Amber's family went out of their way to make her feel welcome. It was so relaxing being with them, because she didn't have to worry about running into someone who might still blame her for what had happened so long ago.

She knew those people still existed in the town, just as she knew Amber's family had never been part of the hate crowd.

Because the invites always included Garrett, Zoey almost felt like Amber was playing matchmaker, but if so, Zoey enjoyed her efforts. It had given her a chance to see Garrett with his family, how he played with the animals, helped out in the kitchen, thanked his sister for a burger, carried Nadine a drink.

So attentive—to everyone.

She'd also run into Garrett at the hardware store when she bought a grill and needed supplies to fix up the house she'd bought. He'd chatted with her, lingering, making her self-conscious over her paint-stained T-shirt and ragged jeans—not that he'd been anything but pleasant.

The owner of the hardware store had slid many suspicious glances her way, but after Garrett came in, he spent his time bragging about Garrett's handyman skills, claiming he'd learned from his uncle Gabe. The owner's wife smiled at him as if he were her own son. They'd talked for maybe twenty minutes, and every minute or so someone new greeted him, including several women. But he hadn't been drawn away. She figured that was likely why the women gave her dirty looks, and not the incident from her youth.

So far, she'd run into him at the grocery, at the ice-cream shop, the gas station and Amber's bookstore. She'd even seen him during one of her many visits to the hospital. Her mother was doing better, but on top of the broken ribs her blood pressure was high and the pneumonia really left her exhausted. Zoey did her best to make her more comfortable, telling her over and over how much fun they'd have once she was well again.

Somehow, she'd make it so.

Garrett was there checking on an older woman who'd almost set her house on fire when she forgot her dinner in the oven. She'd inhaled a lot of smoke, but would be fine.

Such a great guy—and tonight she'd have him all alone, with the opportunity to talk beyond polite pleasantries.

Maybe he'd give her some tips on fixing up her old house, given the amazing job he'd done to his own.

Thanks to a recommendation from Amber, she'd bought the furnished two-story "fixer-upper" sight unseen. And she had no regrets. The second she'd walked across the squeaky wood floors, touched the crystal doorknobs, admired the stained-glass window in the stairwell, she'd fallen madly in love.

The aged, scarred and worn furniture still had charm. Everything—the house and the furnishings—needed a ton of work to spruce it up, and she looked forward to tackling it all. On top of pleasing her aesthetically, it also had a huge sunroom in the back that led to a fenced yard, making it practical for her animal-grooming business.

And when her mother was ready, the spare bedroom with a bathroom just across the hall would work out perfectly. After she'd set up her own bedroom, Zoey had worked on the guestroom, tearing out old wallpaper, using Spackle on the walls where needed and adding fresh paint. She'd decorated with colorful throw rugs, fresh bedding and privacy curtains at the windows.

Best of all, Zoey thought as she opened the gate at the farthest part of the property, the land connected to the lake. She could already smell the water, and filled her lungs with the fresh scent. After moving away, she'd missed swimming, boating, just lazing in the sunshine.

It had taken all of her savings to move back and set up shop here, but so far she was on track to open her business in a few more weeks, and then, with determination, she'd make it all work.

Laying her cell phone, towel and sunglasses in the shade of a tree, she walked out on the rickety dock, tested the water, found it nicely tepid and went down the ladder. Until she knew the depth, she didn't trust diving in.

After working on the house all morning and afternoon, scrubbing walls and floors, cleaning closets, painting trim and making repairs, she needed to cool off and relax her aching muscles.

Along the shoreline, frogs protested, splashing as they jumped in. Once in, she closed her eyes, held her breath and submerged herself in the green water, going down as far as she could to try to reach bottom.

She came up for air, pleased that it was so deep. The wide cove would accommodate a boat, but with a farmer on one side of her, and woods on the other, the area was quiet and peaceful.

Going to her back, she hooked one foot through the ladder and floated, letting the hot sunshine caress her mostly bare body. How long she stayed like that, she couldn't say, but somewhere along the way exhaustion took over and she might have even dozed.

A trickle of cold water on her belly brought her jerking upright with a gasp. She found Garrett crouched down at the end of the dock, his wrists hanging loosely over his knees, an icy bottle of water dangling in one hand. He wore a black cowboy hat tipped back, and a very intent look on his face.

Her foot was still caught in the ladder, leaving her awkwardly thrashing until she freed herself. She went under again twice before finally getting upright. Breaking the surface of the lake, she slicked her hair back and stared up at him.

Mirrored sunglasses kept her from seeing his eyes, but somehow she just knew he was looking at her body, not her face.

"Wanna tell me why you had yourself all hog-tied in the ladder?"

"To keep from floating away."

Voice low, he murmured, "Guess it worked then, huh?"

"Ummm…" Legs kicking as she dog-paddled in place, she squinted her eyes against the glaring sunlight. "What are you doing here?" He hadn't been to her house before.

"Besides taking in the view?"

"Were you?"

"Yeah. For a while now."

Her stomach bottomed out. *How long had he been there?* Had she looked at all appealing…or like a drowned rat? After seeing him so often in town, you'd think she'd be used to his impact.

Not so. He got close, and she went breathless, became anxious and chatty—just as she had in high school.

"Yeah." She cleared her throat. "Besides that."

Straightening, he set the water bottle aside, went for her towel and returned. "Come on out and we'll talk about it."

Zoey blinked up at him.

He stood right there, her towel hanging in his big hand, watching her. And waiting.

Shoot. "I had two suits to choose from," she told him. "A nice, modest one-piece and a bikini. I figured on being alone, so I chose the bikini. Now, though, with you here, I almost feel naked."

"Because you almost are." Unsmiling, Garrett stared down at her…or at least, she assumed he did. Those damned sunglasses hid so much.

Did he look flushed?

She chewed her lip, nodded at his shirt and said, "You could skin down and join me instead." As soon as she said it, her stomach tightened more. Would he? *Oh, she hoped so.*

The barest of smiles teased his mouth. "You trying to get me out of my pants, Zoey?"

What woman wouldn't? She grabbed the ladder for support. "You look—" *hot* "—too warm."

His smile expanded. "That might have more to do with you in that little bit of nothing, than the summer sun."

Her mouth opened, but nothing came out.

"Wish I had more time today, because I think we'd both enjoy it," he continued.

She knew she would.

"Why don't we make that another date? Maybe for my next day off?"

So...he considered dinner tonight an actual date? Not just a way for her to thank him? "Okay."

He checked his watch. "I gotta get back to work soon."

A hint for her to hightail it out of the water. "Right." Besides the hat, he wore a dark blue T-shirt with the fire station logo over the left side, matching uniform pants and a thick black belt with a pager attached to it. It wasn't a uniform, but on Garrett, it had the same effect.

Dropping the towel, he crouched down again and stretched his right hand down to her. "Up and out with you."

Leaving her no choice, she reached up and took his hand. He lifted her, caught her other wrist, too, before she could climb the ladder, and literally hauled her out and onto the dock.

Lake water pooled on the weathered boards below her feet and dripped from her hair, down her arms, her chest, her legs. Uncertain what to do, she stood there beneath the sweltering sunshine in an agony of expectation. When Garrett said nothing, did nothing except breathe deeper and look at her, she decided it might be best if she covered up.

He circumvented her effort to reach for the towel.

"I've got it." Keeping his attention on her, he absently, blindly, bent and snagged her towel before she could.

She waited, but he didn't offer it to her.

Fighting the urge to cross her arms over her chest, Zoey shifted from one foot to the other. Her dark suit wasn't different from what most women wore on the lake. It might even be less revealing than many.

So then why did he stare at her as if he'd never seen anything like it before?

"How long were you in there?" he asked, his voice a little rough.

She had no idea. "What time is it?"

"Three-thirty."

"Oh." She winced. They were supposed to do dinner in two and a half hours and here she was, waterlogged. "Over an hour I guess."

Keeping the towel in one fist, he reached out with the other hand and touched her shoulder, across her collarbone.

That touch made her shiver in reaction.

"You're turning pink. Did you put on sunscreen?"

By dinner she might be even pinker. Her plan had been to cool off, then get in the shade to relax for a bit before preparing for their date. But she didn't want to admit to him that she'd forgotten the sunscreen, or that she'd been so tired she'd all but passed out in the water. "Why did you say you're here?"

There came that suggestive smile again. "I hadn't yet." He moved closer and draped the towel around her shoulders.

Which meant his arms went around her, too.

Standing near enough that she felt the heat of his body, he held the towel closed under her chin. "I need to change our dinner plans."

Well, darn. Hoping to hide her disappointment, she nodded. "Okay." Would he have a good reason to cancel…or had he just changed his mind? "I understand."

"Don't know how you could since I haven't yet explained."

She couldn't think with him so close, his warm hands resting casually above her breasts. "Sorry. I'm listening." *And melting.*

Silence ticked by. "Do I make you nervous, Zoey?"

She shook her head hard in denial and said, "Yes."

Laughing, he released the towel and smoothed her wet hair over her shoulders. "Real clear, honey."

Honey?

Finally, his smiled crooked, he gave her some space.

She almost collapsed with the release of pent-up tension.

Standing a few feet from her, he asked, "Better?"

Heck no. She liked having him close. It was just that close equaled weak-kneed.

Should she admit to being flustered by him when he clearly didn't have the same problem?

"Requires some thought, does it?"

"You don't make me nervous, really, I mean, not usually. But here like this—"

"With you showing all that sexy skin?"

"I…ah…" No way could she agree, because that would sound like she thought she was sexy. "I wasn't expecting to see anyone."

"Can't say I'm sorry I dropped in."

That dark, carnal tone made her toes curl against the rough boards of the dock. "I haven't been in a lake since I moved away. I missed it."

"It's good to have you back."

Like anyone had missed her? Not likely. "If you say so."

He removed the hat, then pushed the sunglasses up

to the top of his head, and oh, God, that was worse. Sweat dampened the front of his shirt so that the material clung to his chest. The hat left his dark hair more disheveled than usual.

And his eyes… His eyes could mesmerize, especially with the sun overhead.

She drew a deep breath and let it out slowly.

Motioning her closer, he said, "Let's move to the shade before you get burned worse."

"Okay." She'd follow him anywhere…wait, what? Shaking her head, she muttered, "You're dangerous."

He gave a soft laugh, shook his head and turned to go to shore.

Zoey quickly readjusted the towel, wrapping it around her body under her arms so that it covered her from chest to midthigh.

He glanced back, and she gave him a bright smile, quickly following.

When they reached the makeshift bench just off the dock, in front of a ramshackle shed, he gestured for her to sit, then sat very close beside her.

He dropped the hat on the ground beside him with the glasses. "I was looking forward to dinner," he told her. "But I'm going to be tied up till eight now."

A hundred thoughts went through her head, and she decided to be straight with him. "You aren't just dodging me?"

Quirking a brow, he looked over her bare legs and shook his head. "Now why would I do that?"

Relieved, she shoulder-bumped him. "So then… you'll have to eat eventually, right? You could just come by here. I don't mind eating late."

He glanced across the wooded property to her house. "You're sure?"

"Actually, I'd love it." He could come at midnight and she'd enjoy it. Knowing she'd sounded too eager, she added, "I was hoping to get your advice on a few fix-up projects anyway."

"Yeah?" He eyed the dock, and then the shed behind them. "You could start down here. I'm surprised either of these is still standing."

"I doubt I'll use the shed for much, and other than worrying for splinters, the dock seems fine." She had more pressing concerns, but she could explain all that to him later. "What's your preference for tonight?"

As he looked her over again, one of his eyebrows went up.

That heated scrutiny sucked the air out of her lungs. "I'm a good cook," she blurted. "Name it and I'll take care of it." God willing, he wouldn't choose anything too difficult.

"You have a grill?"

"That's what I was getting at the hardware store the day we ran into each other."

"The day you wore that messy shirt and had your hair in braids." He tugged on one dripping hank of hair. "You looked really cute."

No way. And here she'd been embarrassed. Feeling her face go hot, she mumbled, "Thanks."

"So if we have the grill, how about I bring some steaks? You can fix whatever you want to go with it. I'm not picky."

She bent a stern look on him. "This is supposed to be my treat so I can thank you."

His attention went to her mouth. “There are other ways you can thank me.”

Whoa. Just like that, a porno played in her head. “Like…what?”

“Not what you’re thinking.”

“Oh.” Disappointment brought her brows down. “How do you know what I’m thinking?”

Abruptly, he turned away.

“Garrett?”

He scrubbed a hand over his face. “I was never going to let you buy dinner.”

Spine stiffening, she repeated softly, “Let me?”

Paying no mind to her indignation, he stood and took a step back from her. “Know how you could really thank me?”

Suspicious, she stood, too—and his attention went back to her mouth.

Heart thumping, she licked her lips. When he groaned, she bit her lower lip.

He drew his gaze up to her eyes. “Sorry.” He worked his jaw. “I do get distracted by your mouth.”

“My mouth?”

Abruptly he said, “You can thank me by going to the fireman’s fund-raiser with me.”

That was so far from what she’d expected that she blinked. “Really?”

“End of the month.”

Plenty of notice. Would she not see him again until then? Cautiously, she said, “That’s a while off.”

“I know you’re busy now getting your house set up for your mom.”

“True.” But that didn’t tell her what she wanted to

know. "I had a lot of stuff shipped here, and I'm still unpacking."

As if he'd read her thoughts, he said, "My days off vary, but I wouldn't mind coming by to help you with the house remodeling if you'd like."

She opened her mouth, but didn't get a single word out before he spoke again.

"I enjoy fixing up old houses, so it'd be a pleasure."

He made it sound like she'd be doing *him* a favor. "I—"

"I work half a day next Saturday so we can get started then, and do a little swimming afterward."

He coordinated dates quicker than she could keep up.

Still looking all too serious, he asked, "What do you think?"

"Actually, I'd love that."

"Which part?"

"Any of it. *All* of it."

"Perfect." He released a pent-up breath and moved in close again. "Now, let's get back to your mouth."

Self-conscious uncertainty had her licking her lips again.

He made a small, hot sound of approval. "Will I be rushing things too much if I kiss you?"

Canting her head, she considered him. He wanted to kiss her, but instead of just doing it, he asked? "I… um…" *Yes, please.* But that'd sound awfully enthusiastic—which she was. "I suppose…"

His hand slid along her jaw so that his fingertips touched the back of her neck. "I haven't been able to think about much other than your mouth."

"Really?"

"Except for when I saw you in the lake." He angled his body near hers. "Then I was thinking about all kinds of things—only some of them having to do with your mouth."

He was so much bolder than she remembered, but of course, he'd been a kid back then.

And he was now a man.

After resting her hands on his shoulders, she hesitated. "I don't want to get you wet."

"Funny." He leaned down until she felt his breath. "I can't say the same to you."

And before she could react to that, he put his mouth to hers, his lips warm and firm, nudging hers open so that his tongue could touch just inside, teasing her own, easing her into things until he had both hands in her wet hair, their bodies pressed together, mouths moving in a hot, eating kiss that obliterated clear thought.

Overhead a crow cawed. Somewhere on the lake, a fish jumped.

When Garrett finally let up, she realized her towel had dropped around her feet. Slowly, he lowered one hand to stroke her naked waist, while his other hand curled around her nape, keeping her right where he wanted her.

She went to lick her tingling lips, but he kissed her again, capturing her tongue and making a sound of pleasure before pulling back.

Still very near her, he whispered, "Even better than I'd imagined."

"You imagined kissing me?"

His gruff laugh teased her nerve endings, but not as much as when he whispered, "I've been imagining it since way back when we were kids in school together."

That surprised her enough that she didn't even blink when he stole another kiss.

"And a hell of a lot more since then."

She remembered Garrett had always been nice to her, but she couldn't recall a time when he'd ever asked her out, or even asked for her number. "I had no idea."

His thumb teased over the corner of her lips. "Now you do." Smiling, he tasted her again, deeper, slower, before reluctantly ending things.

If he'd kissed her like that so many years ago, she wasn't sure she would have left town. "Wow."

"Yeah." He moved his thumb to the pulse thrumming in her neck. "I need to take off, but I'll be here at eight—and I'm already looking forward to it."

In a daze, Zoey watched him snag up his hat and glasses before heading across the yard, his long strides easy, the muscles in his shoulders shifting and moving with each step.

Without much grace, she dropped to sit on the bench again.

If she believed him…well, then, he'd been thinking about kissing her for a very long time.

Odds were, he'd want to kiss her again tonight.

She was naturally an upbeat person, but facing the town again hadn't been as easy as she'd pretended.

Yet now, after Garrett's sensual attention, pure giddiness stole through her, leaving no room for anything else.

For the first time in a very long time, she was flat-out happy. Needing to share, she snatched up her cell phone and put in a call to Amber, her only remaining friend in Buckhorn—even if she was Garrett's sister. By sheer force of will she managed to downplay the kissing aspects and instead focused on her excitement for the coming days.

After her chat with Amber, who was appropriately attentive, Zoey decided to take a quick shower and head to the hospital for another short visit. On her way home she'd stop at the grocery for salad and potatoes.

There were so many changes going on in her life right now, but it was thoughts of Garrett that put the smile on her face and kept it there.

GARRETT HAD JUST finished his general check of the station, making sure everything was clean and orderly. He had a phone meeting in a few minutes, but wanted to grab a Coke before that.

His sister waylaid those plans.

Storming through the station as if she owned it—and sometimes the newbies thought she did—she snagged his elbow and tried to haul him along. There were times when Amber forgot her "little" brother was all grown up, a head taller and a hell of a lot brawnier.

Garrett felt everyone glancing their way, especially Noel Poet, the new hire who'd only recently moved to the area. The locals were used to Amber, but he wasn't sure Noel had ever seen her before.

To see her now, trying to boss him around, wasn't good.

When Garrett stood his ground, Amber's momentum brought her around until she almost slammed into him.

He caught her arm and eased her out of his space, asking calmly, "Problem, Amber?"

Fuzzed up about something, she smoothed her hair, gave a tug to her T-shirt and glared up at him. "I'd like to talk to you in private."

"If you ask real pretty like…"

Instead she tossed back her long hair—as dark as his own—and went on tiptoe, saying in a snarl, "It's about Zoey."

Curiosity ripened in the air.

Not wanting his personal business aired to the station, Garrett took her arm and now it was him leading her off for privacy. She had to double-step to keep up with him.

He took her into the office and closed the door. "Okay, what's the problem?"

Never one to hold back, Amber declared, "You're going to break her heart!"

His brows came down so hard that his head throbbed. "What the hell are you talking about?"

"Zoey!" She slugged his shoulder.

Garrett crossed his arms and propped that shoulder on the wall. "I hit flies harder than that."

The insult rolled right off her. "I didn't want to hurt you. You're supposed to be the good guy."

"I am a good guy." Hell, everyone told him so. "I got her from the airport for you."

"And?"

"And…agreed to let her take me to dinner." After she'd gone from looking pretty nasty to looking like a wet dream. He was still a little shocked by the transformation.

"And?"

"And what?"

"The fireman's fund-raiser?"

Damn, news traveled fast. "Yeah, so?" He had no idea why that had his sister spoiling for a fight. "I figured you'd be glad she had a date." Not that being noble had factored into his motives. "The whole town will be there."

"Right. The whole town—including the Donahues and all their friends."

He scoffed at that. "You aren't saying they'd cause a problem?"

"Oh, my God, where have you been? Living under a rock?"

"They're not that bad." He hoped. But now that she said it…

"When was the last time you saw any of them? They're *always* a problem."

If that was her big concern, she could relax right now. "I won't let anyone insult Zoey."

Rolling her eyes, she gave him a look that said he was hopeless. "Yeah, that'll make her feel better. To be insulted and then have you cause a scene about it."

"I don't cause scenes." He kept a cool head, always.

"Because everyone adores you. But if you'll recall, Zoey left because everyone does *not* adore her. And you two being together will bring up comparisons."

"To her and Gus Donahue?" He dropped his arms and his negligent attitude. "Damn, Amber, that was years ago."

Her attitude softened the tiniest bit. "She's been gone ever since. Her showing up is going to revive that whole nasty bit of history." She held out her hands. "For some, she'll still be the girl from the wrong side of the tracks who brought down the all-star golden boy. And brother, that's how they'll see her with you, too."

He shook his head in denial.

Pitying, Amber sighed. "You know this, Garrett. You know the influence our family has, how others view you as a hero, and how some people can be when it comes to Zoey."

Yeah, damn it, he did.

Even knowing he wouldn't do it, he asked, "Did you want me to cancel on her?"

"You can't. She called me about it because she was thrilled."

Thrilled? He scoffed. "Over going to a fund-raiser?"

"Over being with you."

Yeah, he had to admit—to himself, not his sister—that it thrilled him a little, too. "So she's glad to have a date." Though given how she looked, she probably could've had her pick of men. "It'll be good for her to get around the town if she plans to stay."

Arms crossed, Amber started tapping her foot. "And?"

He wouldn't talk about kissing Zoey. It was private, and none of his nosy sister's business. "And butt out."

Of course she didn't. He wasn't sure Amber could. His sister lived to control the lives of others.

It was one of the things he usually loved about her. She was good at it and could be a terrific resource when vetting dates.

But not right now. Not when it came to Zoey.

"You know it's tough for her to be here, that her mom is in a bad way, that she's trying to start up a new business on top of just buying a run-down house that needs a ton of work before she can bring her mom there. She has her hands full and then some."

Yeah, he did know it. That was one reason he'd offered to help her out—not that he'd tell Amber about it with her being so prickly. Besides, Zoey hadn't acted at all daunted by the pile of burdens. If anything, she seemed eager to take on each and every responsibility. "I saw her house." Then, in case Amber made assumptions, he said, "The outside, I mean."

"Reminds me a little of your place."

"Yeah. Hers could use some TLC, but it's nice."

"The inside is far worse than the outside. Livable, but in need of a lot of repairs."

"That's the way with most old houses." As he rubbed the back of his neck, he thought he saw Amber smile, but the flicker of amusement was gone too fast for him to be sure.

Suspicions gathered like storm clouds as he eyed her innocent expression. Amber was a matchmaker extraordinaire; she always had motives for what she did—including chewing out her brother. "Are you trying to manipulate me?"

She struck an appalled pose. *"Me?"*

What a laugh. "Yes, you."

Checking a nail, she said, "Actually, I put you with Zoey because I thought you'd be least likely to go overboard."

Lightning joined the thunderclouds in his brain. "Overboard…how?"

She dropped her hands. "Face it, brother, you're not Adam."

Insulted without even knowing why, he asked, "What the hell does that mean?"

"He skates through women like it's a sport." She flipped her hand. "And for him, it probably is. He's twenty-nine years old and hasn't once been in love."

Garrett backed up with very real alarm. "You expect me to fall in love with her?"

"Don't sound so horrified. I'm telling you *not* to fall in love with her."

"Wasn't planning to!"

"But you shouldn't sleep with her, either."

He put the brakes on his retreat. "Now wait just a min—"

"Since you're not Adam, who would probably already be in her bed—"

Over his dead body!

"—you should be able to handle that, right?"

No, damn it. He didn't want to handle it. He searched Amber's face, saw she looked dead serious and turned away with a muttered curse.

Since leaving Zoey earlier, he'd thought a dozen times about the way she kissed, how good she'd tasted, the small sounds she'd made, the way those full lips of hers felt under his...

"I can almost hear what you're thinking."

Jerking around, he pointed a finger at her. "Then close your meddling ears."

She pointed right back. "If you sleep with her, then you damn well better step up and be there for her!"

Just what did she mean by that?

Amber slung her purse strap up and over her shoulder and started for the office door. Hand on the doorknob, her back still to him, she paused.

Garrett felt the imminent doom.

"She's not welcome at her uncle's. I don't know if you knew that, but he blames her, too."

Son of a bitch.

"If you've heard the gossip, then you know a lot of people are hanging on to that old grudge."

"You don't," he reminded her. "I don't."

"No." She glanced at him over her shoulder. "You and I also know she deserves better than to be used after walking back into the line of fire for her mom. I hope you remember that, Garrett."

After that direct shot to his lustful intentions, his sister departed, now with less steam than when she'd entered.

Garrett watched her, noticed that Noel Poet did, too. He scowled, but with guilt sitting heavy on his shoulders he couldn't work up any real concern over it. God knew, Amber could take care of herself.

Talk about a turnaround. He'd wanted Zoey, was pretty sure he'd have had her tonight, and he'd figured on them both enjoying themselves.

But he didn't want to hurt her, or add to her burdens. Amber was right—Zoey deserved better than that.

His sister's visit had just changed everything.

Well, hell.

CHAPTER THREE

ZOEY SPENT MORE time at the hospital than she'd meant to. But her mom was awake, feeling more energetic and seemed to enjoy her company. She moved better now, without as much pain. She still had staples in place from the surgery on her hip, and she tired easily from the pneumonia, but she smiled and it gave Zoey hope.

They'd made plans, talking about how it would be when she moved in with Zoey, and for the first time since her return, her mother's eyes had glittered with anticipation instead of pain and defeat.

How could she leave in the middle of that? She couldn't, so she'd stuck around until the very last minute, then had to race to get to the grocery store so she'd be back at her house before Garrett got there.

Funny thing though, as she raced the cart down an aisle, she recognized his sexy butt in worn jeans.

He stood at the meat aisle checking out the steaks.

Zoey snuck up behind him, considered patting that fine tush, but decided against it with so many people around. Her rep was bad enough without adding fuel to the fire.

Instead, she gave him a hip bump. "Hey, stranger."

Garrett turned with a big smile that, for some reason, faded as he saw they had an audience. "What are you doing here?"

She could ignore the gawkers, if he would. "I was visiting with my mom, so I'm running late. Sorry. Just grabbing some salad and potatoes and heading home."

He snagged up a package of steaks, commandeered her cart and steered them both back in the direction she'd just come from. "How's she doing?"

"Much better, thank you. They'll have her up and walking soon." She eyed the enormous steaks.

"I meant to hit the butcher's, but a meeting ran over and they closed a few hours ago. Luckily the grocery stays open all night now." He hustled her along as he spoke. "You remember how they used to roll the sidewalks up at six?"

"Yes." She tried to slow him down. "Where are we going?"

"You said you wanted salad."

"Isn't it back that—"

"Zoey Hodge."

Oh, God. That particular screech of outrage carried the same effect as it had in high school. Zoey cringed, knew Garrett saw her cringe, and belatedly realized why he was taking her the long way across the store.

He'd hoped to spare her, but it was bound to happen sooner or later.

Taking two seconds to compose herself, Zoey put on a friendly smile and turned to face the unpleasant past. It wasn't just Carrie. She had her younger brother—Cody—with her. They both gave her venomous glares.

"Carrie," Zoey said with calm, polite regard. "How have you been?"

As bitter as ever, Carrie crowded into her space, narrowed her eyes and hissed, "How dare you come back here?"

As they stood by the grill, for the tenth time, Garrett asked, "You sure you're okay?"

His concern was sweet, but it was starting to get laughable. "Do I look broken?" She rolled her eyes, hoping he'd let it go. Yes, it had been ugly. Cody had watched her with sad, narrowed eyes. And Carrie had looked…haunted.

She felt a little sick being the recipient of all that ugly emotion.

But she hoped she'd handled well.

Certainly, she'd handled it better than Garrett. She could still hear him saying, *High school is over, Carrie. Grow up already.*

The poor girl had stood there looking mortified, wounded and vindictive all at the same time, until Cody had quietly led her away. Clearly she'd expected Garrett to back her up.

That he hadn't made Zoey almost feel sorry for her.

His hand clasped her shoulder. "The Donahues are only a small part of the community."

"I know." In high school the Donahue children had been part of the elite society. But even before Gus had died and Carrie started openly hating her, Zoey had been an outsider. Her lower-income upbringing and the free-spirited way her mother raised her had ensured she'd always be different. She couldn't remember a time when she'd ever belonged.

Freaks, Carrie had told her, belonged nowhere.

Zoey told herself that most people were happy to move beyond a seven-year-old scandal. "A lot of people here have watched me with some uncertainty, but overall they've been nice." She stepped around Garrett to turn the steaks. "And your family, of course, is always awesome."

"Yeah, they are." He took the long fork from her and removed his steak from the grill, plopping it on a platter.

Distaste scrunched her face and her stomach curled. "You're going to eat it that bloody?"

"It's rare," he explained.

"It's still *mooing*."

He laughed, took in her aversion and paused. "Does it really bother you?"

"Yeah. I'm not sure I can kiss someone with blood on their teeth, and I really wanted to kiss you again."

As if someone had used the fork on his sexy butt, he jumped—then froze.

Case in point, Zoey thought, knowing she'd again spoken out in a way few would have. But darn it, she had no skills in tact or subtlety. "You don't want to kiss me again?" Because she was pretty darned certain he did. And she definitely wanted him to. Shoot, her lips still tingled from that earlier taste.

His gaze went to her mouth, held there, and he groaned.

Now what was that about? Did he regret kissing her? Hands on her hips, she frowned at him. "Is something wrong?"

"Not a thing." While muttering something about his sister, he put the steak back on the grill.

Unsure if that meant he would kiss her after all, she moved nearer to him. When he faced her, her heart tried to punch its way out of her chest. "Amber eats her steak raw, too?"

"Rare, and no. She's medium." He stroked her hair,

seemed to catch himself, and tucked a stray tendril behind her ear. "What about you?"

"I'm well-done. No pink at all."

He opened his mouth…then shut it again with a wince of guilt and focused on his steak, using the long fork to move it to the corner of the grill.

"What?" Zoey goosed his midsection, realized there was no give to the solid muscles there and opened her hand on him for a better feel. He felt *really* good under the soft cotton of his T-shirt. "What were you going to say?"

"Something I shouldn't." He caught her hand and held it.

"Okay, now I have to know!"

"It was…" He glanced at her, did a visible struggle with himself and gave up. "Suggestive."

"Suggestive?"

"Sexual," he clarified.

"Really?" Better and better. She leaned in and lowered her voice. "Tell me."

With a wicked smile, he gave in. "Something about me liking pink." When she just stared at him, he elaborated. "Pink. On you."

She shook her head.

And that made his smile widen into a grin. Bending to her ear, he whispered, "I think of pink, and I visualize all those warm, damp places on your naked body—"

"Garrett!" With a rush of heat—not all of it embarrassment—she stumbled back from him.

Amusement growing by the second, he shrugged. "You insisted."

When he had her blushing, he seemed more comfortable, like maybe her embarrassment presented a necessary barrier between them. "I don't understand you."

"I'm a guy. Easy enough to understand."

She snorted. Nothing easy about him at all. He teased and flirted, but was most at ease when she didn't return the favor. Did he flirt with every woman? Maybe she read too much into it. Maybe it made him uncomfortable to know she was equally—or probably more—attracted to him.

He lifted the steak. "Is that cooked enough that I can eat it without repulsing you?"

It wasn't, but she nodded anyway.

She didn't have a picnic table yet, or even any outdoor chairs. But it didn't bother Garrett. Before starting the grill, he'd gone to his truck, got a blanket from behind the seat and spread it in the yard picnic-style beneath one of the tall elm trees.

It was by far the most wonderful, romantic dinner she'd ever had.

By the time they started eating, the sun had sunk low, barely visible behind the hills, splashing the sky in inspiring shades of crimson, tangerine and mauve. The air cooled a little, making it more comfortable even as the nighttime humidity set in.

They ate in a cozy silence, watching as lightning bugs showed up by the dozen. Zoey plucked a blade of dewy grass. "I'd forgotten how damp everything is around a lake. I'm getting wet just sitting here."

This time when he grinned, Zoey knew why and she threw her napkin at him.

With a low laugh, he tossed it back at her. "Don't want me to visualize that, huh?"

"No!"

"Too late," he said softly. Reaching out, he caught her ankle and moved his thumb over her skin. "Are you this soft all over?"

At that brief, simple touch, her heart sped up. "I don't know."

Their gazes clashed and held as his fingertips trailed up her calf to the inside of her knee.

Her heart hammered and her toes curled.

Abruptly he released her, pushed his empty plate back and left the blanket to explore the fire pit a few yards away.

Staring after him, Zoey saw the stiff way he held his shoulders. Why the sudden retreat?

"Have you used this yet?"

"No." Quickly she finished up the last few bites of her own meal and joined him.

It felt very intimate standing beside him in the shadowy sunset. All around them insects chirped as twinkling stars pierced the dark sky.

Zoey didn't want the evening to end already. After clearing her throat, she asked, "Can we fire it up, do you think?"

He crouched down and examined the stones placed around the pit.

While he did that, she examined the breadth of his shoulders, the long line of his spine, how his thighs strained the denim of his jeans.

No two ways about it, the man was put together fine. But her draw to him was more than that. He'd always been friendly, a natural-born leader, and now as a fireman he lived as a hero. He had an easy, comfortable way about him that proved he made up his own mind instead of being swayed, didn't judge others, but instead offered help when he could.

She thought of how he'd defended her in the grocery store, and it did funny things to her. Nice things.

Turbulent things.

For the longest time he remained in that position, his face turned away from her.

Tension mounted until Zoey doubted she'd be able to convince him to stay. "Garrett?"

He straightened again, and looked down at her for a heart-stopping length of time.

She smiled. "You okay?"

"Yeah." Almost against his will, he touched her cheek, then shook his head. "I'll gather up some kindling if you want to grab matches and maybe some old papers, too."

"All right." But to be sure, she asked, "You're staying a little longer?"

"If that's okay."

"It's terrific." Lighthearted now that she knew she hadn't chased him off, she collected their dishes on her way in and put them in the sink. Her ancient plumbing didn't include a dishwasher, so she'd take care of washing them later.

While inside, she hugged herself, anticipating more kissing.

Garrett kept her guessing, but she'd learned to live with optimism.

After locating an old magazine and the box of matches she kept with candles on a shelf, she hurried back out.

It pleased her to see that he'd rearranged the blanket and their drinks closer to the pit and had an impressive stack of twigs laid inside it, with some bigger fallen branches waiting to go on next.

"Will this work?"

"That's perfect." He tore out several pages, rolled them tightly, and stuck them between the twigs.

Unsure what else to do, Zoey lowered herself to her knees on the blanket.

And hoped he would join her soon.

While he worked, he asked in more detail about her mother's progress and seemed genuinely pleased that she was doing better. Because his work as a fireman included paramedic training, he had a great understanding of what her mother's treatment would be.

"I should be able to bring her home by the end of the month. Until then, I still have a lot of stuff to get done inside."

"Before I leave, I could take a look."

"At what?"

He laughed. "Your house. That way I'll have an idea of what we need before we get started next Saturday."

Sitting back on her heels, Zoey considered him and his repeated offers to help. Was he just being his usual terrific self, or looking for reasons to be around her?

Everyone knew his entire family was made up of do-gooders who took large, active roles in the community, either through their careers, or plain goodwill. Being that he was the same, maybe Garrett saw her as a project.

She hated that idea.

Once the fire started, Garrett added a few of the bigger logs, waiting until they snapped and hissed before sitting beside Zoey. Legs out, arms braced behind him, he sat catty-corner to her, facing the fire.

She faced him, her knees almost touching his thigh.

"That shed is a fire hazard," he said. "I think we should just knock it down."

"I peeked inside there one day, saw a snake and haven't gotten anywhere near it since."

"I'll take care of it."

That made her frown. She put her shoulders back. "It's my shed, so I'll help. Even if there are snakes."

He gave her a fleeting smile. "All right."

Damn. She glanced at the shed in the dusk and shuddered. Maybe she should have kept her mouth shut.

"So, about your mom…" With noticeable caution, he asked, "Think she'll be up to joining us at the fundraiser?"

Thrilled at the suggestion, Zoey stared at him. "You're serious?"

"It's a big event. Most of the town will be there. I mean, it's not like it would have been…"

"Private?" The way this was.

"Yeah. There'll be competitions and dancing and raffles. What do you think?"

The firelight played over his face, putting blue highlights in his hair, emphasizing the cut of his cheekbones, the length of his dark lashes. She sighed. "I think you're wonderful."

That must have surprised him. His brows twitched with a puzzled frown. "You don't mind?"

That he was sweet enough to include her mother? "Of course not." Without thinking about it, she leaned in and gave him a quick, tight hug of gratitude. "Thank you."

She started to lean away again, but with his left arm around her, he kept her close. His hand opened on her back, caressing. He nuzzled her temple.

Relaxing, she sank against him.

Near her ear, he murmured, "You smell good, Zoey."

She loved hearing that particular husky tone from him.

The heat of the fire teased along their skin, combating the humidity. Down by the lake, frogs started a chorus of croaking that echoed over the yard.

When he did nothing else, she asked, "Are you going to kiss me again?"

"Do you want me to?"

She pressed back to see his face. "That's a joke, right?"

He smiled. "I'll take that as a yes."

Zoey held her breath...and then held it some more while Garrett appeared to struggle with himself.

Starting to feel insulted, she quirked her mouth. "If you don't want to, I won't pressure you."

"You can't pressure me." He held on to her when she would have pushed away. "And what I want isn't the problem."

"Then do it."

His gaze dipped to her mouth.

Exasperated, Zoey huffed, leaned in and smashed her mouth over his. That spurred him into action and he took over, slowly adjusting to make the kiss softer, deeper, nudging her lips to open so he could lick his tongue inside.

One hand tangled in her hair, the other curved low on her back, very near her behind.

Zoey wrapped her arms around his neck and held on. She wouldn't mind kissing him for, oh, a week? He tasted good, smelled good and felt even better.

Easing back, he kissed the corner of her lips, her jaw, up to her ear.

Zoey rasped, "See. No problems."

She felt his smile against her jaw. "You'll give me a tour of the house?"

Unsure of his motives, she measured her words. "I'd love to show you around." They'd be inside…near her bed.

Was she ready to go there so soon?

Once her mom came home, the opportunity might be lost, so…yes. She was ready, especially after that heated kiss. "Just keep in mind that relocating and buying the house and starting up the new business is straining my savings, so I'm doing things as—" *cheaply* "—affordably as I can."

"Not a problem. Labor is usually the biggest cost." He nipped her bottom lip. "But I'm affordable."

Would she need to pay him? And how would that work?

Another quick, firm kiss, and he sat back from her. "Stop fretting, Zoey. We'll work it out."

"I almost never fret. It's pointless." And thinking that, she dropped to her back on the blanket to take in the inky sky glittering with stars. "Look at that."

Garrett said, "I'm looking."

"It's such a clear night." When he didn't comment, she asked, "You don't enjoy the stars?"

She sensed more than heard him moving closer before he said, "I do."

"I swear they look different here than they did in the city."

"That's where you lived?"

"When I left here, I wasn't sure where to go. I just

wanted…out. But I ended up in Lexington, and it suited me. I had a cute little apartment, a terrific job as an assistant with a pet groomer, plenty of friends…"

"That you didn't mind leaving?"

What could she tell him? Lexington was great—but it wasn't Buckhorn. "As Dorothy would tell you, there's no place like home." And she'd missed home so very much.

He came down on his elbow beside her, near enough that she felt the warmth of his body and could breathe in his scent. "You should never have gone away."

Turning her head, she tried to see his thoughts, but the flames of the fire danced, distorting his features, making him look almost…apologetic.

But that didn't make any sense. He'd had nothing to do with her situation back then.

Quietly, she said, "You know I had to."

"I know the rumors. I heard the gossip. You broke things off with Gus Donahue, and he didn't take it well."

Her short, harsh laugh disturbed the quiet of the peaceful night, and she quickly apologized. "Sorry. It's not funny—but what an understatement. His reaction was so over-the-top, I didn't know what to do."

His gaze drifted over her, her face, then her body beneath the moonlight. "Would you tell me what actually happened?"

There had been few opportunities to talk about that wretched event. She'd confided only in her mother because there'd been no one else interested in the truth. "You really want to know?"

"If you don't mind telling me."

As if the words had been bubbling near the surface,

just waiting for permission, she blurted them out. "Gus wanted to have sex, I didn't, and he flew off the handle."

Garrett didn't seem surprised, and he didn't doubt her. "I can understand him trying. You were hot even back then."

She blinked at him. Garrett had thought her hot?

"But even a horny kid has to understand that no is no."

"He said I'd led him on and that the whole town would call him a fool if he couldn't score with someone like me."

Garrett was silent—but he touched her, first her wrist, the back of her hand. He traced her fingers, then laced his in hers, palm to palm. His big, strong hand engulfed hers, emphasizing the differences in their sizes and giving her an added thrill. "I'm sorry."

"About what?"

"How unfairly you were judged when no one had the whole story."

She shrugged it off; she'd long since grown used to the biased assessment of what had happened that day. Even so, it felt nice, really nice, having someone to hold on to. "It wasn't the first time that he'd gotten enraged over something ridiculous. I'd had enough of it, and I told him we were through."

"That's when he left?"

Remembering, she gave a slow shake of her head. "First he broke a few things. One of our lamps, my mom's music box." Her chest hurt with the memory. "It had been her grandmother's, and it sat on a shelf in our living room."

Garrett lifted her hand, kissed her knuckles.

That small kiss held encouragement and understanding, spurring her to tell it all. "He…he shouted and cursed, called me some vile names and punched the wall right by my head. He hit it hard enough to leave a big hole there, and his knuckles were bleeding."

Garrett went still.

"It terrified me, and that made me furious." To explain that, she said, "I always lose my temper when I'm scared."

"That's better than giving in to the fear."

"I guess." A damp breeze drifted over her skin; here, now, with Garrett, she felt exposed and vulnerable, but not in a bad way…which made no sense at all. "I pushed him away and told him to get out and never come back. It was like I flipped a switch. He went from furious to sorry and pleading." Her breath caught. "He begged me to forgive him."

"But you made him leave anyway."

"Yes."

He kissed her knuckles again. "That was the smart thing to do, Zoey."

"It didn't feel smart after he died." Her stomach cramped, remembering the devastating news, the guilt that had all but smothered her.

"What happened after he left wasn't your fault. *None* of it was your fault."

Seeking a measure of calm, she pulled away from his hold, folded both hands behind her head and focused on that big, star-studded sky. It was easier than looking at Garrett. "That's not how everyone else saw it. I went from being a nobody to being public enemy number one."

"That's not true."

"Close enough." Had he scooted nearer somehow?

He seemed to be looming over her. She kind of liked it. "It wasn't easy coming back here."

"You're strong and brave."

Laughing, she slanted him a look. Yep, definitely closer. "You like to see the best in people." The moonlight and firelight competed to emphasize all the most appealing angles of his face, the width of his shoulders, the bulge of his biceps. She sighed. "If it weren't for my mom, I wouldn't have come back. Ever."

"I'm sorry she's hurt," he whispered. "But damn, Zoey, I'm glad you're here."

GARRETT HAD DELIBERATELY chosen to eat outside with her, thinking it would be safer than being indoors…near a bed. But seeing Zoey like this, relaxed, sharing, with the stars shining above her and her clear enjoyment of nature, well, it was worse than having a bed nearby.

It was heated foreplay, and he felt himself reacting.

Filtered through the leaves of tall trees, the moonlight played with her body, slipping over the swells of her breasts, the length of her thighs.

It'd be so easy to lean down to her, to kiss her…and more. To let his hands explore all that warm, dewy skin.

Even while he fought with himself, his breathing deepened and his muscles tensed. The shorts she wore teased him, exposing so much and concealing so little. And that V-necked T-shirt, dipping low to her cleavage. Every so often when she moved, he saw the edge of lace on her bra and it drove him nuts.

Each time he saw her, he discovered something new about her, something nice, or enticing, or…lust-inspiring. Without seeming to try, she reeled him in with open smiles, silly conversation and her big heart.

In many ways she was such a dichotomy—strong and accepting, ready to tackle the past and future alike. But so soft, too, her hair, her skin, that peek of lace… and her attitude toward others.

He didn't want to be a sap, but her emotional generosity really got to him. He'd never known a woman like her—sympathetic enough to help care for a sick kid, understanding in the face of insults.

Even Carrie, with her nasty reception and hateful barbs, hadn't been able to dent Zoey's natural compassion. He'd been furious with Carrie and Cody, but Zoey had been calm and thoughtful.

"You're so quiet," she whispered. "What are you thinking?"

Her light brown hair, baby fine, fanned out around her head, drawing his fingers. "I'm having a hard time not kissing you."

"Oh." She dropped her gaze to his mouth. "You can, you know."

Encouragement was the last thing he needed, because he knew the truth even if she didn't. "Kissing will lead to more."

"Like…?"

Laughing a little roughly, he sat up and turned away from temptation. *Remember what Amber said, remember what—* "Like how I'd love to get you out of those shorts." The words left his mouth and he wanted to kick his own butt. From the moment she'd come downstairs from his shower when she'd arrived in town, every instinct he had as a man told him to go after her.

To get her.

He wasn't used to fighting himself. Before Zoey, it had never been an issue.

Zoey said nothing, and the silence condemned him. She hadn't been back to town that long, she had a full plate, and here he was pressing her for sex.

As soon as he got himself together he'd apologize.

Just the fact that he had to collect himself proved his reaction to Zoey was different. As a firefighter, he'd learned to stay calm no matter what.

As a man, that personality trait had come naturally in all relationships.

Now he felt far from calm. He couldn't recall the last time he'd been this physically and emotionally drawn in.

Yet his meddling sister had to go and spell out a dozen legitimate reasons why Zoey should be off-limits for casual sex.

He heard the rustling of her movements as she came to her feet, likely to call an end to the evening—not that he could blame her.

With the apology forthcoming, he turned—

And Zoey unzipped her shorts.

He froze, every muscle clenched tight as he waited, watching her, anticipation burning hot.

She pushed the shorts over her hips and let them fall to her ankles.

God, she was gorgeous.

She stood there with her T-shirt rumpled, her hair messy, wearing that same sexy pair of panties that she'd dropped in his driveway.

"Well?" Twisting her fingers together, she whispered, "Say something already."

He had no words. Scooping an arm around her behind, he tugged her closer and pressed his face against her, kissing the bared flesh of her belly between the bottom of her T-shirt and those minuscule panties that barely covered her.

She felt smooth and soft, smelled indescribably good. He opened his mouth against her skin for a gentle love bite, then soothed the spot with his tongue while tasting her warm skin. He wanted to devour her. Every inch of her.

Right here in the open yard.

Moaning out a soft sound of acceptance, as if that plan worked for her, Zoey sank her fingers into his hair and held him closer.

In that moment, Garrett had no doubts; right or wrong, he'd already reached the point of no return.

CHAPTER FOUR

SLIDING A HAND around to her shapely ass, Garrett cuddled her closer. He wanted to touch her everywhere, all at once, and he wanted more of her mouth.

God, her mouth.

He easily levered her weight, lowering her to the blanket again.

"Wow," she whispered. "You're strong."

"You're small. And sweet." He slid his gaze down her body, over her breasts to her belly, lower. "And so fucking hot."

Drawing in a shuddering breath, she watched him. "I've never heard you talk dirty."

"It's a wonder I can talk at all." Sitting back to look at her, he said, "I'm on the ragged edge here." Looking wasn't enough, so he opened a hand on her flat belly. Breathing deeply, he trailed his palm up to the dip of her waist, pushed the T-shirt up over her ribs, all the way to her bra.

Zoey surprised him by sitting up, grabbing the hem of her shirt and jerking it off over her head. "You, too," she ordered.

He obliged, stripping off his shirt and tossing it by hers.

With purring interest, she put her small, warm hands against him, spreading her fingers out over his chest.

He brought her in for another taste and, keeping his mouth on hers, lowered her to the blanket once more. He was aware of the crackling fire, the sounds of nature.

And Zoey.

Each small sound she made, each shiver and gasp, made him want more.

He was content to enjoy her mouth for a good long while, each kiss hotter, longer.

Damn, the girl could kiss.

When she pushed him to his back, he went willingly, enjoying the way she sprawled over him, how she stroked his shoulders and chest and down to his abs.

When her busy hands reached the front of his jeans, he went still. "Zoey..." he rasped in warning.

"Mmm?" Sitting up, she tackled his snap and carefully, agonizingly, lowered the zipper.

Like a sexy angel, she knelt beside him, the firelight making a halo of her tangled hair. Muscles pulled taut in anticipation, he watched as she slipped a hand inside his fly...and stroked along his length.

Groaning, he tried to think of all the reasons why he shouldn't let her rush things. But damn, with her hand working him, rushing seemed like a very good idea.

He was dying to see her, all of her, so while she stayed occupied making him insane, he reached for the front closure of her bra.

It opened easily, the cups parting to show soft, full breasts and tight, pink nipples.

Zoey removed her hand long enough to shrug off the bra, leaving her naked except for those sinful panties. Before she could go back to tormenting him, Garrett sat up to remove his shoes and socks, then stood to shove out of his jeans.

Still on her knees, now in front of him, Zoey said, "The boxers, too."

He had no problem with that and shucked them off as well.

Like a living fantasy, Zoey gave another vibrating *"mmmm,"* and reached for him.

A smidgen of reality wormed in past the smoldering lust and Garrett caught her hands. "Hold up a second."

Staring up at him, her green eyes big and—*damn*—hungry, she whispered, "Why?"

It took a lot of fortitude on his part, but Garrett came down to his knees with her. Getting the words out wasn't easy, but for Zoey, he managed. "Are you sure about this?"

"Definitely."

Her answer came too fast for him to take it seriously. "You haven't been in town that long—"

"I'm ready."

"—and I'm rushing you."

Laughing, she toppled him backward so that she was on top again, her light brown hair forming a curtain around them. "Are you always this hesitant about sex?"

"No." God, no. He loved sex. Always. "I want you to know that you're different." As in special, damn it.

"Really?" Even though she sounded impressed by that, she squirmed on him, shattering his resolve. "That's sweet."

"Zoey." Garrett curved one hand to her jaw, the other to her ass, trying to keep her still. "I can wait if you need me to."

"Well, aren't you superhuman," she teased.

Damn straight, because that's what it took to be noble with her.

"The thing is…I'm not." Zoey lightly bit his bottom lip. "And it's been a long time for me." A sweet, barely there kiss on his chest. "And I'm ready now, as in *right now*." To emphasize that point, she moved against his straining erection. "Once my mom is here, I won't have much opportunity for stuff like this."

Was she already putting a time limit on their relationship? Like hell. Sure, her mom would need some help, but they'd figure it out.

"So please," she said, giving him another little nibble, "no more talking—unless it's to say something naughty or enticing. You know, to turn me on more." She trailed her hot little tongue along his ribs, and lower. "Not that I need it, because seriously, Garrett, I'm there."

When her mouth teased over his hip, he gave up. Again.

"Do you have protection?" she whispered.

He could feel her hot breath. "Yeah."

"I figured." She closed both hands around him, nuzzled against him and he knew, flat-out knew, if he felt her mouth on him, he'd never be able to hold out. They'd have to save that for later, when he wasn't coiled so tight.

Catching her forearms, he dragged her up his body so he could take her mouth again, then turned her under him. "My turn."

"But I wasn't done."

"Any more of that and I would've been."

"Oh." Satisfaction curled her lips.

Sweet, silly Zoey.

"I think I'd like that," she whispered. "Pushing you to lose control."

He cupped her breasts. "I'll look forward to it. Later

though, okay?" Lowering his head, he drew in one nipple, pleased with the way her back arched, how her breath caught, the clench of her fingers in his hair. He kept it light, suckling gently before moving to the other side. He drew her in, harder this time, and moved his hand down to her panties.

She lifted into his touch, her breathing ragged. Finding her panties already damp pushed him dangerously close to the breaking point.

Insane. He loved to tease, building the pleasure, but now, with Zoey, he felt consumed with the need to get inside her.

Hoping she was ready, he moved his fingers inside the material, stroking over her, parting her and finding her silky, wet and hot.

"Garrett, *now.*"

"This?" he teased.

She held her breath when he slowly worked two fingers into her, pressing them deep, keeping the heel of his hand firm against her.

"Now," she insisted on a gasp.

"Soon," he whispered.

She clamped around his fingers, and he felt new moisture slicking his hand. "Now, now, *now*—"

Her urgency spurred his own. It took him only seconds to snag up his jeans and locate a condom. Eyes heavy, Zoey watched him tear open the foil packet and roll it on. He reached for her hips, snagging his fingers in the waistband of those sexy little panties.

With more haste than finesse, he tugged them off. She wanted him to rush, but he needed to take a minute just to look at all of her. "Damn, you're sexy."

"Flattery will get you everything."

It wasn't flattery, just truth, but she kept curling her toes and shifting, and he knew she was in the same shape as him.

He liked that she wanted him so much, that she felt the same chemistry.

"Garrett?" Her breasts trembled with her broken breaths. "Don't be a tease."

Smiling, he settled between her legs, then said, "Kiss me, Zoey," doing what he could to hold off, wanting it to last.

She did, but went one further. When her slim legs wrapped around him, her ankles locking at the small of his back, Garrett groaned his surrender.

He adjusted, positioned himself…and slid deep.

On that very first thrust, she cried out. Knowing sounds carried on the lake, he kissed her, and kept on kissing her even while riding slow and deep. She matched him in every way, countering with a roll of her hips, holding him tighter and tighter.

Given how quickly she started coming, she'd been even closer to the edge than him. Those sweet, internal contractions milked him, her heated scent enveloped him, and she arched hard, putting her head back on a harsh, high moan.

That did it for him.

Pressing his face against her neck, he gave in to release, still rocking into her until all his tension eased away.

He thought to keep his weight off her, but Zoey hugged him tight, so he carefully settled atop her.

Her long sigh of satisfaction made him smile—until he felt her stiffen. "What's wrong?"

"I think I heard something."

A second later, he heard it, too.

ZOEY HAD BEEN adrift in utter bliss, her limbs still tingling, the weight of Garrett's hot, hard body offering a very unique comfort.

Until a rustle in the bushes to the right pulled them apart.

She stared into the darkness. "What was that?"

Eyes narrowed, Garrett said, "I don't know." He pressed a hand to her shoulder. "Stay put."

"I'm *naked*," she reminded him in a panicked whisper.

"Not like I'd forget." He handed her T-shirt to her and pulled on his boxers and jeans.

She watched him. "What did you do with the condom?"

Even with firelight making the shadows dance, she saw the incredulity in his glance.

"Sorry," she whispered. "But I've never done this outdoors thing before."

Just as quietly, he said, "Tossed it in the fire."

"Oh." Ingenious. As he started to step away, panic set in. "What are you doing?"

Keys rattled when he pulled a key chain from his pocket with a small flashlight connected to it. "Checking on things."

She said, "Oh," again.

Garrett shone the low light over the tall weeds…and they both saw the movement.

Her heart hammering, Zoey quickly yanked on her panties. "Probably just a critter," she said hopefully.

"Not a raccoon or possum," he said. "Too big."

Too big? The weeds moved more, parted…and a pair of eyes reflected off the beam of the small flashlight. She nearly swallowed her heart. "That's not a snake, right?"

"Stay still," Garrett told her.

She went one further and held her breath…until the dog came slinking out.

Oh, thank God.

"Hey," Garrett said softly to the animal. "Easy, boy."

Zoey almost melted. How could Garrett be so freaking awesome *all the time?* Few men could transition from incredible stud to stalwart protector to gentle caregiver without a hitch. Being so gorgeous was just overkill.

"He's limping."

Her heart softened more, this time in pity. "Looks a little rough around the edges, too. Poor guy." Very slowly she got to her feet and pulled on her jeans.

Watching them both, the dog held back.

"No collar," Garrett said, moving the flashlight over the mutt. "He's loaded with ticks, a few scratches—"

"And that limp."

"Yeah." He went down to one knee. "You okay, guy? How friendly are you?"

That Garrett didn't just try to run the stray off was almost enough to melt her knees. "Will you be okay here with him if I go get some food?"

"Yeah, but go slow."

"I know." She'd been around animals all her life. A hurt animal might take any sudden movements the wrong way. So she didn't run, but she didn't dawdle, either.

In the kitchen, she snatched a plastic bowl off the

shelf and quickly emptied an entire package of bologna into it. On her way out, she turned on the back porch light. It helped only a little.

Garrett was now within a few inches of the dog, his hand extended.

If anything, the dog looked worried.

And desperate.

She was still a good distance away when he started sniffing the air. Smiling, she held the food out in front of her as she eased closer.

"Let me," Garrett said, reaching back so she would hand the bowl to him.

The big protective lug.

"I know what I'm doing," she reminded him. "I'm the expert."

"Groomer," he countered, but he didn't interfere when she very slowly set the bowl down in front of the dog.

"Does that mean you want to pick the ticks off him?"

"Want to? No. But I'll help." Taking her hand, they both moved back to let the dog eat.

He emptied the bowl in a few big, noisy bites.

Zoey studied him, the small, mostly tan body with black and brown markings, the floppy ears, the soulful eyes. "He looks like a beagle-Jack Russell mix."

"Still young," Garrett agreed.

Now that the dog had solved one problem, it inched closer, sniffing.

"No more just yet, sweetie." With apology, she said, "You'll get sick."

Garrett touched under the dog's chin, and he let him. As if that broke the ice, the poor little thing limped closer, his tail thumping with hope.

Tears turned Zoey's vision blurry. "I'm taking him in."

Garrett smiled. "I already knew that."

TRUE TO HIS WORD, Garrett stayed and helped. It was past midnight by the time they had the dog tick-free, bathed and a nasty thorn removed from between the pads of his front right paw.

Zoey put out fresh bedding, then put up a gate at the kitchen doorway. "Hopefully I can get a vet appointment tomorrow."

"My uncle Jordan will fit him in."

She'd forgotten that his uncle was a vet. "You don't think he'd mind?"

"He'll insist." Crossing his arms over his chest, Garrett propped a shoulder on the wall. "I can meet you there first thing tomorrow morning if you want."

So sweet. Smiling at him, Zoey stroked his biceps. She would never tire of touching him. Or looking at him. And hopefully more. Lots more. "If you're free and want to join us, that's fine. But if you're busy, I can handle it."

Now that the dog was clean, had eaten again and was given a fresh dish of water, he looked exhausted. After only a few cautious glances their way, he went to the corner of the kitchen where Zoey had made his bed, dug around, rearranged things, snuffled and kicked, and finally, after turning two circles, dropped down with a lusty sigh.

Garrett's grin pleased her as much as the dog's acceptance. She hadn't planned on taking on even more responsibility, but the dog was here, and she'd make it work somehow.

"I like your house."

Drawn from her thoughts, she looked around, seeing what he saw—cabinets that needed to be sanded and painted, cracked linoleum floors, watermarks on the ceilings.

His hands settled on her shoulders. "Every old house needs work. That's part of the fun."

She wondered if he really meant that. For her, it would be fun because it wasn't just a house, it was a new beginning. "I'm looking forward to it. But the kitchen won't be the first room." She took his hand and started down the hall. "I've already done some work on my mother's bedroom and bathroom, but I'd love your input on what still needs to be done."

The dog slept on undisturbed. He must have really been tired. Thinking of him wounded and all alone tugged at her heart. But never again. She'd make sure he had enough love to recover.

As they went through the modest house, Garrett offered nice compliments on every room she showed him. Like her, he focused more on the unique qualities of the older home, instead of what needed to be done. She loved that he felt the same as she did about it.

Midway through the tour he suggested she get a pen and paper so they could make notes and figure out what was needed.

"You're sure you don't mind?" Zoey didn't want to take advantage of him. He'd already put in a full day, then helped her with the dog. "It's getting really late."

He touched her cheek. "Tired?"

With him around? "Not me."

"Good." His thumb went under her chin, he tipped

up her face and gave her a short, soft kiss. "Let's make a list."

For another thirty minutes they went over everything, and Zoey felt like she had a good handle on which updates were priorities and which could wait.

Even better, Garrett insisted he'd enjoy helping out as often as possible.

When they reached her bedroom, he stepped inside and looked around with interest.

Being there with him, near her bed, meant there was no way she could keep her thoughts on repairs. He'd already given her an incredible orgasm, but now…

Now she wanted more.

"The room looks like you."

That made her laugh. "Peeling paint and scuffed floors? Gee, thanks."

He nodded at the bed. "Soft blankets, everything tidy but colorful." His gaze met hers. "Inviting."

Such a wonderful compliment—though she seldom thought of herself as tidy. "Thank you."

"For?"

"Everything." Lifting a hand, she gestured at the house, at the pet hair and muddy paw prints clinging to his dark shirt. "For the kind words, the encouragement and advice, and for helping out with the dog."

He didn't move from his position near the bed. "Is that my goodbye for the night?"

"What? No." She closed the space between them. Unsure of how bold she should be, wary of chasing him off, she said, "I was hoping for more kissing?"

Humor lit his eyes. "Is that a question or a fact?"

"Both?"

Smiling, he shook his head. "You don't protect yourself at all, do you?"

"From you? Why would I."

Indecision took him across the floor—away from her—but he came right back again. Determination stopped him in front of her. "You were phenomenal."

"Really?" She grinned and lifted a fist. "Go me."

"The thing is..."

Uh-oh. "What?"

"I can't be anything more than a friend."

They were already more than friends. Or, having had her once, was he satisfied? "You don't want me anymore?" She must not have been all that phenomenal after all.

His eyes flared, then narrowed. "Of course I do."

"Then what's the problem?"

"I'm not looking to settle down anytime soon."

Insult, disbelief and incredulity kept her staring at him for far too long. Should she laugh, be indignant? Or just be honest?

He stepped closer. "Zoey?"

Honesty won out. "Here's the thing, Garrett. I just got back to town, right? My mom is having *all* kinds of health issues. I'm trying to open up a new shop and make enough of a living to support not only me, but her, too. So far as I can tell, a third of the town doesn't remember why I left, another third remembers but doesn't care and that last third is still harboring some animosity."

"I'm sorry."

She waved off the apology. The last thing she wanted was his pity. "Do you really think I have the time or the inclination for a committed relationship?" He started to speak but she cut him off. "Because I *don't.* Actually, I'm pretty beat."

"I didn't mean..."

"And really. Sex once doesn't lock you into anything." She tried a cheeky grin. "Sex twice or three times still doesn't count as a promise, not to me."

This time when he started to speak, she put her fingers against his mouth.

"If you want to be friends, yeah, that'd be great—as long as it's friends with benefits because I'm too busy to clear my calendar just for an occasional chat or fast food. But sex? At my convenience, and yours of course, now that I can work out. So what do you think?"

He knotted a hand in his hair, looking a little frazzled. "About?"

"Weren't you paying attention?"

"I think so, yeah."

"So how about more kissing? And maybe more... everything else, too?"

CHAPTER FIVE

GARRETT BLEW OUT a breath. "Honest to God, Zoey, you make me a little nuts."

She pursed her lips. "Should I apologize?"

He laughed. He didn't mean to, but damn, she was about as unique as a woman could get. "Don't apologize, and don't change."

She eyed him. "I don't understand you."

"Okay, so understand this—I'd like nothing more than to spend the whole night kissing you." The *whole night*—what the hell was he saying?

"Yes."

He'd been about to retrench, to make excuses on why he had to go, but her unguarded enthusiasm made him feel like a coward. While he shied away from his emotions, she embraced hers without reserve.

He knew the truth; in a very short time he'd come to like her too much, think about her too often.

Want her in ways that were only in part sexual.

Would it be so bad if he let things progress naturally? Now that he'd had her, now that he knew how good it was between them, how could he walk away? Especially given that she claimed to feel the same.

And if they grew tired of each other…how could there be hurt feelings when right now, she didn't have the time or energy for more anyway?

"You're pondering things far too long," she complained. "I have my pride, you know. If you'd rather just go, I promise not to kick up a fuss."

That made up his mind. "It was dark outside."

"Just the firelight, I know."

"I'd like to stay. With the lights on so I can see you better."

Her eyes widened.

"And no threat of mosquitoes or echoes off the lake."

"Echoes." She covered her mouth. "I hadn't even thought of that." Then with a grimace, "Was I loud?"

"You were so damned sexy, I didn't get a chance to linger as long as I wanted. You started moaning all deep and hot and I lost it."

She beamed at him.

"Let's check on the dog, take him out one more time, then I could use a shower before we turn in."

"A shower—with me?"

"I was going to ask." Damn, she pleased him. For now, he'd put his sister's guilt trip from his mind and take things as they came.

One day at a time—starting tonight.

SEVERAL DAYS LATER, Garrett was outside with the guys on a quiet, sunny afternoon washing the engines when Amber came to visit him again. She and Zoey were friends, so no doubt she knew how much time he'd been spending at Zoey's house.

Was she here to give him another lecture?

He rolled his eyes at her purposeful, long-legged stride across the lot…until he realized Noel Poet had zeroed in on her, too.

Deciding now might be a good time to let the new

guy know of family connections, Garrett headed over to meet her halfway. "Amber."

She gave him a double take, then matched his formal tone. "Garrett."

Putting an arm around her shoulders, he led her to where Noel, shirtless and with his pants soaked to the knees, ran a soapy sponge over a rescue truck. Or more to the point, he held the sponge near the truck. With his attention clearly elsewhere, he wasn't doing much in the way of actual washing.

When they approached, Noel swiped a forearm over his face and then just waited until they'd reached him, his eyes narrowed against the sun.

He stood an inch or so shorter than Garrett's six-two. During a recent tour with the elementary school, Garrett had overheard two of the teachers whispering about Noel's dark blond hair and lean, muscular body. At the time he'd found it funny and had harassed Noel over it later.

Now, with his sister looking at Noel, Garrett wasn't sure how he felt about it, mostly because he'd heard other things, too.

Like how Noel got around, how he enjoyed variety and how he planned to stay single.

When they reached him, Garrett said, "Amber, this is Noel Poet. He's new to the station. Noel, my sister, Amber."

Surprise lifted Noel's brows. "You're intro-ing me to your sis? Seriously?"

Damn it, did the man have to make it sound like he'd just thrown Amber on the sacrificial altar?

Amber smiled and stuck out a hand. "Nice to meet you."

Smile slow and suggestive, Noel transferred the sponge to his other hand and swiped his palm along the seat of his pants before taking hers. "Might've been nicer if you weren't related." He kept the handshake brief.

Garrett worked his jaw. "I figured since she comes around often enough—usually to give me shit about something—I might as well introduce you."

Amber leaned in to Noel—which made both his brows go up—to say in a loud stage whisper, "I only give him a hard time when he needs it."

"Which she seems to figure is twice a week at least."

For one brief moment, Noel's gaze dipped over her before he caught himself. "The family resemblance is there," he told them both. "Wish I'd noticed sooner."

Amber's smile brightened more. "Hope you don't hold that against me."

Both men stared at her. Garrett because he'd never seen her flirt, and Noel, well… Garrett knew exactly where the man's mind had gone—and it had to do with holding body parts against her.

Frowning, Garrett took her upper arm. "I'll let you get back to it."

Noel nodded and murmured, "Guess I should," but he continued to look at her.

Uncomfortable for a variety of reasons, Garrett led Amber toward the garage and relative privacy.

"He seems nice."

No, he didn't want Amber thinking that, but if he tried telling her what to do, she'd do the opposite just to prove a point. "So what's up?" he asked, hoping to divert her.

She took the bait. "You and Zoey."

"Yeah?" He'd definitely been *up* that morning. The night before, too. But right now, here at the station, he had it under wraps.

That is, unless he started thinking about her too much.

"You didn't take my advice," Amber said.

"Advice?" His sister was never that understated. "You mean your order for me to leave her be?"

"Semantics." She walked over to a tool chest and seated herself. "Zoey said she's gotten more done on the house in the last week with your help than she would have in a month on her own."

"Yeah, so? I'm good at repairs."

"Sounded to me like you've been there nearly every day."

All but one, not that he'd give her details.

Amber stared at him.

"Stop it."

Failing at the innocent look, Amber asked, "What?"

"You're patiently waiting for me to spill my guts." In the past, that silent stare might have worked. But not since he'd hit his twenties. "My relationship with Zoey is none of your business."

"So it *is* a relationship?"

An awesome, hot, sexually inspired relationship, which he also enjoyed when they weren't having sex… but he didn't want to dwell on that too much. Things were happening fast. Mach-speed fast. He wasn't sure how he felt about that, and he had no clue how Zoey felt about it.

She loved sleeping with him, that much he knew. And she smiled a lot while they worked on her house.

He often found her watching him with a really sweet expression on her face.

But he didn't know what that expression meant.

Amber pushed to her feet in a rush. "I ask, because Zoey just assured me that it wasn't."

As usual, when he started thinking about Zoey, he got distracted. "Wasn't what?"

"A relationship."

Ire quickly replaced the confusion. "You were gossiping about me?"

Flapping a hand, she said, "Save that deadly tone for someone who intimidates more easily. I'm your sister and you know I would defend you with my dying breath."

Mouth twisted over that dramatic statement, he repeated, "Dying breath, huh?"

"Of course." Smiling, she added, "Because I love you."

Oh, hell no. "You're up to something."

That made her laugh. "I'm just trying to get a lay of the land."

Noel walked in to grab some dry towels. No one said a word, but Amber tracked his every step, making Garrett frown again. When Noel walked back out, whistling, Amber released a breath.

"So are you or are you not interested in her?"

Sneaky, jumping right back to the topic that way after she'd just ogled a fellow firefighter right in front of him. But how could he answer? He was far beyond interested. Bordering on obsessed. On the downhill slide to falling in love.

He knew it, but that didn't mean he'd share with Amber.

"Never mind." She patted his chest. "I know you well enough that I can see for myself."

He caught her arm before she could leave. "What did Zoey tell you exactly?"

"That you guys were having fun in a no-strings-attached way that worked perfectly for her because—" Amber coughed "—the perks were awesome."

Nice. "She didn't go into the perks?"

"She enthused until my face was so hot I had to leave." After sticking her elbow in his ribs, she said, "A little brother should never be described as a stud. That's not a direct quote, by the way. Zoey was far more descriptive than that."

Garrett grinned.

Amber didn't. "So now, instead of worrying about Zoey, I have to worry about you." She shook her head. "A sister's job is never done."

"Why would you worry about me?"

"Oh, Garrett. You don't know? The bigger they are, the harder they fall."

He wouldn't fall alone, damn it. Zoey would come around. Right?

"If you're rethinking that no-strings-attached nonsense, you ought to clue Zoey in real soon. Once her mom comes home and her responsibilities double, she just might have to prioritize her time."

And Amber figured he wouldn't make the list? Or was she trying to manipulate him again? He'd bet on the latter. "We're taking it one day at a time."

"I know." She looked at him with pity. "And that means that tomorrow could be very different from today. You might want to keep that in mind."

This time when she started away, Garrett let her. Damn it, he'd been in such a great mood, and now…

Now he felt the need to make himself more invaluable to Zoey. He'd start on that tonight. If by the fireman's fund-raiser she hadn't come around, well, then he'd state the obvious to her.

The obvious being that they were good together, and that he fit into her life, whatever her life might be.

But until then, he'd rather give her a chance to tell him how she felt. He'd encourage her at least once a day…and every night.

LEAVING THE BED unmade—why bother?—she and Garrett repeatedly bumped into each other while dressing. It wasn't the limited space so much as she couldn't keep her eyes off of him. Fully dressed he was a visual treat. Naked…yeah. She wasn't missing that for anything.

While trying to step into her shorts, she tripped herself up and would have fallen if Garrett hadn't caught her.

"Let me." Going to one knee, he eased up her shorts… while kissing her thighs, her belly, each breast.

She braced her hands on his hard, wide shoulders and sighed.

Though they'd just finished making love, he murmured, "I need another hour."

Or a lifetime.

Her eyes popped open. Oh, no, where had that thought come from?

"Zoey?" He slowly stood, towering over her. "Everything okay?"

He'd spent the night again.

He stayed over almost every night.

And it was so wonderful that now she wondered how she'd ever be able to sleep again without him spooning her, holding her close. He worked with her, played with her, talked with her… He'd invaded her life in so many ways that now he seemed very much a part of it.

"Zoey?"

She tried to nod yes, but the answer was no, and she ended up sort of waggling her head in a totally indecipherable way.

Garrett grinned. "You are so damned cute." He kissed the end of her nose, then pulled her T-shirt over her head, smoothed her hair back and just held her face. "Are you worrying about your mom?"

"A little." That wasn't an outright lie. She worried about her mom all the time. "I want everything perfect for her when she comes here."

Garrett sat on the end of her bed and pulled her down onto his knees. "Can I ask you something?"

"You can ask me anything."

"What does your uncle think about your mom moving here? She's been living with him, right?"

"He's okay with it."

His big hand smoothed over her back. "Amber told me you weren't welcome at your uncle's."

Ducking her head, Zoey wondered how to explain. "He's still a little mad at me." As soon as she said it, she felt Garrett's anger. It was funny, but she could read him so easily. "He thinks I never should have left her. And he's probably right."

"Know what I think?"

She tucked her head under his chin and breathed in the warm, masculine scent of his big body. "Yeah, I do."

He tipped up her chin, forcing her to meet his eyes.

"Why didn't your mom or uncle back you up way back then?"

Seeing him like this, caring, concerned for her, well, she had to kiss him.

He didn't disappoint her.

Kissing Garrett would never grow old. But when she came up for breath, he said, "Will you tell me?"

There was really no reason not to. "My uncle wanted me to stay and defend myself."

That surprised him. "He didn't blame you?"

She shook her head. "Everyone assumes that. But he'd dealt with Gus and knew about his temper. He said he tried to help him work it out in football, but… he wasn't a very happy guy. It made my uncle furious that, as he put it, I was just going to turn tail and run. Especially since that'd leave my mom…alone."

As if he knew she needed it, Garrett hugged her tighter.

"Mom is the quintessential free spirit, always has been. She loves me a lot. Back then, I was her whole world. After dad died when I was twelve, she never dated."

"She just focused on you?"

"Pretty much." Zoey didn't want it to sound like her mother was weak, even if that was partially true. "She'd never worked outside the home, so she had a hard time holding down a job. That's why we were always so poor."

"Your uncle was counting on you to help her make ends meet?"

"And to be there for her." She opened her hand on Garrett's chest, toying with his chest hair, savoring the heat of his skin. "When I left, Mom just…gave up. That's why my uncle had to take her in."

"You were a kid, Zoey. Your uncle should have known you couldn't be responsible for your mom."

"That's the thing, though. I had been, ever since Dad died." She tipped back her head to see him. She needed him to understand. "Now I will be again."

"Now you're a grown woman and she's hurt. Family helps family, always."

"Yes."

"Which is why she should have been helping you back then."

The truth hurt, but she nodded. "Maybe, but she can barely help herself." As soon as she said it, she winced. "I'm sorry. A daughter shouldn't say something so awful about her—"

"Shh." Garrett pressed his mouth to her temple. "It's just me."

Just him—the only person she could really share with. Not to another living soul had she ever criticized her mother. "I love her."

"Of course you do."

He kissed her again—her ear, her cheek, the corner of her mouth—and she accepted the truth. Damn it, after all her assurances, she'd still fallen for him.

"So your uncle won't be a problem?"

"No." Loving Garrett…now that might be a problem. But not her uncle. "He's annoyed still and holding a grudge. But he'll come around because he'll want to visit Mom, and he knows he has to behave when he's here."

Rough fingertips glided gently over her jaw. "You're something else, you know that?"

"Yeah?" She smiled up at him. "Like what?"

He started to reply, but Ticket, as she'd named the dog given the number of ticks he'd had on him when she'd first found him, went into a barking fit.

The dog only barked like that when something scared him.

"You expecting someone?"

"No."

Garrett set her on her feet and started through the house.

She hurried after him. "What are you doing?"

"Seeing who's here."

She trailed him to the front door, where Ticket kicked up a fuss, bouncing up and down and howling like hell had come to call. "You think he heard someone?"

"Ticket is smart." As soon as he patted the dog, Ticket sat down and stopped barking. "See?"

"But I don't get any visitors." And maybe that's why Garrett looked so protective.

He opened the door…and there stood his father with his fist raised to knock.

The two men stared at each other, and Zoey felt her face go bright red.

After all, it was the butt-crack of dawn, she was badly rumpled, and Garrett wore only jeans. No way could his father misinterpret.

Trying to brazen out the embarrassing situation, Zoey said, "Mr. Hudson, good morning!" She peered around Garrett's bare shoulder. "How nice of you to visit."

Garrett choked.

Morgan, big beast of a man that he was, gave a slow

grin and clapped his son on the shoulder. "I'm not going away, so you might as well invite me in."

Silent, Garrett stepped back, opened the door wider and gestured for him to enter.

Ticket, the little rat, was the only one thrilled for the company.

GARRETT CALLED THE station to say he was running late, pulled on his shirt, socks and shoes and joined Zoey and his dad in the kitchen. He got there just as the coffee finished.

Giving one last pat to the dog, his dad gave him the once-over. "I was just telling Zoey how nice the place looks."

Garrett glanced at her, saw the high color in her cheeks deepen and had to smile. "We've been working on it."

"You don't say."

"Dad." He accepted a mug of coffee from Zoey and handed another to his father. "You're embarrassing her."

They both looked at Zoey, and she froze.

"Oh, no," she spluttered. In a too-high voice, she said, "I'm fine," and froze again.

Garrett pulled out a chair for her, urged her into it and bent to kiss the top of her head. "You remember my dad, Zoey?"

She bobbed her head hard. Reacting to her uncertainty, Ticket sat next to her chair and kept a watchful eye on things.

Yeah, Morgan Hudson had that effect on a lot of people. He'd been sheriff for a long time, and if the stories Garrett had heard were true, a bad-ass longer than that. Few realized that overall, his dad was a big softie.

Not that anyone would believe him if he told them so. In his early sixties, his dad was still a brick wall of a man: tall, solid, unfaltering in his role as protector.

All in all, the best of dads.

"He used to be the sheriff back when we were kids," Garrett told Zoey. "Now he's the mayor."

She bobbed her head again. "I know. Amber caught me up."

"I knew you were a friend of Amber's." He nodded at Garrett. "Didn't know about this, though."

"Dad…" Garrett warned again—not that it would do him any good.

After sipping his coffee, Morgan asked, "You remember me as a fair man, Zoey?"

"Of course."

"Good. That'll make this easier."

Garrett wondered if they'd dealt with each other back when Gus died. Likely. For as long as he could remember his dad had been a pillar of the community. Whenever something happened, Morgan Hudson was there taking control and working out problems.

Was it a problem that had brought him here today?

Muscles tensing, Garrett put a hand on Zoey's shoulder. "Don't let him make you nervous."

"No, of course not." Her smile was about as nervous as it could get.

His dad gave him that look, the one that said all kinds of shit a son didn't want to hear, especially when he was full-grown and well past needing lectures.

"Did Amber send you here?"

Folding his arms on the table, his dad said, "No, why would she?"

"No reason." Interesting, that Amber hadn't told their

dad about him seeing Zoey. Maybe she still had hopes of him backing off.

If so, she was doomed to disappointment.

Garrett straddled his own seat. “So then why the visit?”

Instead of answering, he told Zoey, “I’m here on unofficial business. Do you want Garrett here, or would you rather talk privately?”

Stiffening from his toes to his ears, Garrett scowled. “I’m not going anywhere.”

“Not up to you,” Morgan told him.

Garrett turned to her…and saw her stricken expression. “Zoey?”

Eyes closed, she whispered, “Someone complained about me being here?”

“Complained—and made some accusations.”

“The Donahues,” Garrett growled. Damn it. What was wrong with those people?

Morgan ignored him. “I’m here as a courtesy, okay? To *you*, not them.”

She nodded, swallowed. “Thank you.”

“You’re going to open shop?”

The switch threw her. “Pet grooming.” Straightening her shoulders, she met Morgan’s gaze. “Everything is legal, all my permits in order, everything to code.”

He looked around again. “I assume you plan to live here, too?”

“With my mom.”

Garrett had no doubt Morgan already knew about her mother being hurt, but he briefly filled him in anyway. “She should be able to come home by the end of the month.”

“I’m glad she’s doing better.”

“Thank you.” Zoey shifted with impatience. “I don’t mean to be rude, but why are you here exactly?”

After turning his coffee cup, giving himself a moment to think, Morgan looked at each of them. “There was some trouble at the grocery?”

Dropping back in her seat, Zoey laughed.

Garrett didn’t. “I was there.”

“Really?” Raising his brows, Morgan said, “I must’ve missed that part.”

“I don’t want any trouble,” Zoey said. “Not with anyone. I’m just here to take care of my mom.”

Garrett felt a pang in his heart. Yeah, he knew that was why she’d returned. But hopefully she’d want to stay…for him.

CHAPTER SIX

INSULTED ON HER behalf, Garrett took Zoey's hand. "I can tell you exactly what happened." While explaining how well Zoey had handled the ugly confrontation, he felt incredible pride. "Because I knew it might be uncomfortable for Zoey, I was already leading her in the opposite direction. Carrie caused the confrontation, and she was damned nasty about it, too."

"I don't doubt it." Morgan finished off his coffee. "The Donahues aren't great at taking blame."

Zoey didn't understand. "Blame for what?"

Garrett shared a look with his dad. "Anything." A lot of people thought the Donahues needed to spend more time parenting and less time excusing bad behavior.

She shook her head. "If you didn't buy in to the accusations, then why are you—"

"To give you a heads-up that they might cause more trouble. I thought you were out here all alone." Now he looked at Garrett. "It's an isolated piece of land. Not far by car, but the nearest neighbor is a good two miles away."

"I have a phone," she reminded him.

"Storms knock out reception all the time."

Wearing an indulgent expression, Zoey asked, "Are you trying to scare me?"

"A little fear is a good thing."

She laughed. “It’s not like the Donahues are psychos, or like Buckhorn is a hotbed of crime.”

“No,” Garrett agreed. “But we have had the occasional problem.”

“And putting the Donahues aside, any woman alone in an isolated place has to use extra care.” He looked at Garrett. “Until you get some security lights up and maybe an alarm system, it wouldn’t hurt to have some company.”

Meaning he should stick around and ensure her safety? Garrett had no problem with that. He wanted to be with Zoey, and no way would he let anyone hassle her.

But damn it, she’d spelled it out—her plate was full and she didn’t have time for anything more involved with him. He was already pushing his luck staying over so often. If he got too intrusive, it might spook her.

As Amber had said, he could be the first responsibility she shook off.

His dad, though, didn’t seem to have the same concern. “Should I take it you’ll be around some?”

“Some,” Garrett said through his teeth.

Which only made Morgan grin. “You know that youngest Donahue boy has a tendency to get in over his head.”

“Yeah.” He did know it. And in fact, he had some suspicions when it came to Cody Donahue.

“I personally think he’s looking for attention, but—”

“I know. Tough to get through to Mr. and Mrs. Donahue.”

“I can take care of myself,” Zoey suddenly interjected with emphasis.

Garrett hadn’t realized she was gathering steam until

he looked at her. Then he saw the stubbornness, and the independence.

She said she'd been looking after her mom since her dad died. By now she probably thought she didn't need anyone.

He'd have to find a way to convince her otherwise, but without being too obvious. "It can't hurt to take extra precautions."

Without looking at him, she said to his dad, "Thanks to the work Garrett's done here, the locks are all up-to-date. And of course, I have Ticket."

The dog jumped up to her lap, looked at Garrett and then at Morgan and let his tongue loll out.

Laughing, Morgan sent Garrett a look that said *I tried.* He pushed back his chair. "If anything comes up, let me know."

Setting the dog back on the floor, Zoey stood, too. With a lot of suspicion, she asked, "Is that the job of the mayor?"

"Around here, everyone seems to think everything is my job."

"I don't."

"Because you're new, I reckon." Morgan bent to give the dog a few more strokes. "But in this case, I head up the COCP program."

"Community organized crime prevention," Garrett explained. "Basically it's made up of residents and local agencies working together on crime, delinquency, vandalism, that sort of thing."

"You're part of it?" she asked him.

He nodded. "Shohn, too, since he's a park ranger."

"And Adam keeps an eye on things at the school." Morgan shrugged. "When everyone stays in touch with everyone else, things get figured out sooner rather than later."

Covering her face, she muttered, "The whole town is going to be in my business."

"Part of the charm of Buckhorn County," his dad told her with a squeeze to her shoulder. "Nice dog, by the way."

That got her to stop hiding behind her hands. "Thank you. He's wonderful."

As if he understood her, Ticket started wiggling all over again.

Morgan smiled. "I think you'll do a real nice business here, Zoey. Jordan already told me you have a way with animals."

His uncle Jordan had liked her on the spot. Anyone who took in a stray won him over, but Zoey was so sweet, who wouldn't love her? Sick babies, stray dogs… every guy with a pulse.

For certain, he wasn't immune.

Damn it.

While Garrett struggled internally, his dad started for the door, so he and Zoey followed with Ticket bounding behind them.

"The nearest groomer is a county over. You'll be more convenient, and the setup looks great—for a business. Living out here, though…" Concern still showing, he said again, "Be extra careful, okay?"

Before Zoey could answer, Garrett put his arm around her. "We will."

Amused at his obvious predicament, his dad grinned. "If you need any help advertising your grand opening, give a yell." He paused with the door half-open. "You'll be at the fireman's fund-raiser?"

"Garrett invited me and my mom."

"He did, huh?" His dad raised a brow. "Guess we'll all get to know you better then—if we don't have a chance to visit before that."

Which was code for *you should have brought her home for dinner already*, and *your mother is going to kick your butt if you don't take care of that real soon.*

"In fact, I'm betting the majority of the town will greet you warmly." His gaze met Garrett's. "The men are all real friendly that way."

When Garrett worked his jaw, his dad added, "The women, too, of course."

Nodding, Zoey said, "Thank you again, Mr. Hudson."

"Call me Morgan." He drew her in for a hug, winked at Garrett and finally left.

Garrett checked the time. He was going to be even later than he'd figured on, but he knew what he had to do.

He caught Zoey's shoulders. "We need to reconfigure our plan."

"Our plan?"

Meaning to keep it light, he kissed her—but yeah, that never worked with Zoey. Half a minute later, both of them breathing deeply, he said, "That whole business of taking it one day at a time?"

"What about it?" She pushed back from him. "Are you changing your mind just because your dad is trying to pressure you? I'm still fine with us just being friends."

He'd moved beyond the friend stage a day after meeting her. Now he just needed her to catch up. "Friends who have sex day and night."

She gasped in accusation. "You don't want to have sex anymore?"

Silly Zoey. Did she really think he could give that up? Give *her* up? "I want it to be exclusive."

She snapped her mouth shut.

Garrett dared another kiss, and managed to keep that one under fifteen seconds. "The longer you're here, the more people you'll meet." And his dad was right; guys would hit on her at the fireman's fund-raiser. "You and me," he said with insistence as he started away. "Friends with benefits, as long as we're only benefiting each other."

He gathered up his hat and his keys, and stooped to say goodbye to Ticket.

When he straightened, Zoey still stood in that exact spot. Did being exclusive scare her so much?

He tipped up her chin, and this time said more softly, "You and me."

Eyes huge, she bit her lip, and finally, *finally*, after torturing him with a long, searching stare, she gave a small nod. "You and me."

Progress, he thought.

One day at a time.

ZOEY AWOKE SUDDENLY, aware of Garrett sprawled beside her. Given the shadows in the room, it was super early still. They'd be doing the fireman's fund-raiser later, but they still had time.

Trying not to disturb him, she turned her head and took in the sight of his long, strong body. On his side facing her, his hairy thigh against her hip, his hand curved over her naked breast, he remained deeply asleep.

His long, thick lashes hid those incandescent blue eyes that never failed to melt her heart. Rumpled dark hair just added to his sexiness, as did the whiskers on his jaw.

She wouldn't mind waking next to him every day for the rest of her life.

Lately, things had been…surreal. Better than she'd ever known was possible.

After demanding that exclusive agreement—and really, who would she want other than Garrett?—he'd decided she needed to spend more time with his family, too. Not just the cousins, but his parents, his uncles and aunts. They were all so welcoming, treating her not as the town pariah, but more like someone very special.

He'd also made several trips with her to the hospital to visit her mother. Once he even stopped by without her, dropping off flowers that had put a smile on her mother's face for days.

Her house was now freshly painted, many repairs done and her business was ready to open. She still had some big projects to do, but thanks to Garrett—*oh, Garrett*—all the plumbing worked, the electrical was safe and the dock had been rebuilt.

He was just plain amazing. Tireless when it came to lending a hand.

Or sex. He was especially tireless then.

She didn't know how a guy could be more wonderful.

Ticket felt the same, always greeting Garrett with howls and a thumping tail when he got home from work. It warmed her heart, how much the dog loved him.

And it scared her a little, because she was starting to feel the same.

The hand on her breast moved, cuddling a little…and it was no longer just his leg she felt on her hip.

"You big faker," she whispered. "You're awake."

"I felt you looking at me." Still without opening his eyes, he brushed his thumb over her nipple, making her shiver. "What time is it?"

"I don't know." She twisted to see the clock…and instead found Ticket standing beside the bed looking at her.

She'd long since removed the gate in the kitchen, giving the dog the choice of where to sleep, but he repeatedly returned to the same spot where she'd first put him, what she and Garrett now referred to as Ticket's corner.

As soon as the dog saw her move, he barked.

Groaning, Garrett released her to stretch. "I take it he wants out."

Usually that would get a resounding yap from Ticket. Not this time.

He growled, reared back on his haunches and whined.

"What the hell?" Garrett sat up, looked at Ticket and threw back the sheet. "Something's wrong."

Having the same feeling, Zoey took only one second to admire Garrett's body as he yanked on jeans, without underwear. She grabbed for her housecoat, but Ticket was already racing down the hallway, barking in excitement, before she'd even gotten her arms in the sleeves.

Without waiting for her, Garrett followed him.

"Damn it." Zoey hastily pulled on panties then tied the belt to the housecoat. Figuring she was decent enough, she ran after them.

Gray dawn struggled through the fog, leaving too

many shadows in the yard. The morning mist in the air kept the porch light from traveling very far.

With Ticket hooked to his leash, Garrett stepped out with him…and saw the smoke coming from her ramshackle shed.

He thrust the leash at Zoey, said "Stay here," and took off. Barefoot. Into the darkness.

And possible danger.

"Damn it," she said again, more meanly this time.

Ticket had a fit, jerking and pulling at the leash when she went back in for a flashlight and her phone. It took her less than a minute, but when she got back outside she saw her small shed engulfed in fire.

And there was Garrett, backlit by the flames, leading a reluctant Cody Donahue toward the house.

Oh, no. Just what she didn't need.

Her heart sank, especially when she got a good look at Cody's face. The boy was lost, and if someone didn't intercede, he could end up with the same needless fate as Gus.

Blowing out a long breath, Zoey knew she'd have to take on one more responsibility.

And it was going to be a doozy.

When Garrett reached her, he said in a voice as placid as the lake, "Don't let Ticket loose, okay? The fire should burn itself out, especially with everything still dew-wet. But we don't want him near it."

Straining away from Garrett's hold, Cody avoided her gaze.

She held the door open for both of them.

Like her, Ticket watched with quiet sympathy until they were inside, then he started sniffing the grass.

Zoey gave him plenty of time to do his business…

while also giving Garrett plenty of time to do his. She assumed he'd call the sheriff, maybe the fire station… she wasn't sure, but there'd definitely be some confusion going on.

When Ticket finished up, she went into the kitchen. With the phone to his ear, Garrett stood behind Cody, who sat at the table. He had a hand on the boy's shoulder, and to Zoey the touch looked more like reassurance than restraint.

When she caught part of the conversation, she knew it was Cody's father Garrett spoke to.

"This was a courtesy call, Mr. Donahue, that's all."

A raised voice came over the line. Garrett waited, occasionally giving Cody a squeeze.

"No, you may not come get him. He'll be at the sheriff's station." Garrett nodded. "Sure, call your lawyer if that's what you want to do. No, I'm sorry, but there's no mistake." Again he squeezed. "I caught him myself, Mr. Donahue. He still had the lighter in his hand."

Zoey unleashed Ticket, who decided to lay by Cody's chair, then she went about making coffee. She and Garrett finished up at the same time.

To give them some privacy, she said, "I'll go get dressed."

He nodded, and then to Cody, asked, "You drink coffee?"

"No."

"Want a cola then?"

Stubbornness and suspicion hunched his shoulders. "I guess."

"Don't run," Garrett said when he released him. "It'll only piss me off and this is bad enough already."

"I wasn't going to."

Feeling far too emotional, Zoey went on down the hall. By the time she'd dressed, the deputy had arrived, along with a fire truck and Morgan Hudson. The yard was busy, the kitchen busier. And all she could think about was how Garrett had handled Cody.

He hadn't bullied him, or hurled accusations. He'd been compassionate but firm.

God, she loved him. Like crazy, over-the-top, never-going-to-end love.

In for a penny, she decided… She'd do what she could for Cody.

And then she'd do what she could for herself…with Garrett.

THE MORNING WENT by in a blur and Garrett stayed so busy he didn't get a chance to see Zoey after leaving the house with the deputy. He'd showered and shaved at his own place, and barely gotten to the fund-raiser on time. Now, behind a booth grilling corn on the cob, games all around him, a dance stage set up across the way, his thoughts divided a dozen different ways.

Number one, he wanted to throttle Cody's dad. The man had made a big production of insisting Cody was innocent no matter the evidence, no matter Garrett himself being an eyewitness. When his rude blustering got him nowhere, he turned on Cody, loudly complaining that he didn't have time to waste on nonsense.

Cody's dad was so opposite his own that Garrett couldn't fathom what it must have been like for him growing up. Losing a brother, having a father who made excuses, but didn't take time for him.

That led him to number two, because he wanted to take Cody under his wing and maybe help him see a better way. Cody needed to know he wasn't a waste of time. He could still make amends and get on a better path before he hurt himself or someone else. Though he thought for sure it was Cody responsible for the fire by the lake, and no doubt in the woods, too, he hadn't been busted on anything else. With a little guidance, he just might be able to get it together.

And thinking of better people led him to number three. Zoey. He wanted to cement their relationship, to have her actually commit to him. He wanted that bad.

A few minutes later, there she was, wearing a pretty sundress and sandals, her silky brown hair dancing in the breeze. Garrett set aside his tongs and watched her sway to the loud music blaring over the park. Did she dance?

He wouldn't mind holding her to a slow song when he got a break.

Her mother was in a wheelchair pushed by her uncle. They paused at a booth to get colas, smiling and taking in the crowd. Zoey bent to say something to her mom, smiled at some kids running past and pointed at balloons.

Garrett pushed back his hat, his heart already tripping. She had that effect on him. Every single time.

Moseying along with her mom and uncle, she searched the crowd. When she saw him, she stopped dead in her tracks. Color rushed into her cheeks and she sank her teeth into that plump bottom lip. Two seconds later she put her shoulders back.

Huh.

After saying something to her uncle, she started toward him.

Wondering what she was up to, Garrett nudged Noel, said, "Be right back," and left the booth.

He met Zoey halfway across the main entrance to the park. "Hey."

"Hey." Clearly keyed up about something, she stared at him. "Do you have a minute?"

The serious way she asked that left him uneasy. He searched her face. "Is something wrong?" Was she still upset over the fire that morning? "I can rebuild the shed, you know."

A smile flickered. "I know. It's fine." She poked him. "At least the snakes are gone, right?"

"You live in the woods, honey. There will always be snakes."

Wrinkling her nose, she said, "Thanks. Just what I needed to know."

"Forget about snakes. You're upset." And trying to hide it. "What's going on?"

She shored herself up with a big breath. "This morning, when I saw you with Cody Donahue, I made up my mind. About two things actually. And because you'll want to come home with me again after the fundraiser—"

"Damn right I will." Someone bumped into him. He glanced back and saw the line for the corn had grown. Noel looked harassed, especially with the music even louder now.

"Come here." He moved them both away from the growing line and noise and, to be clear, stated, "I *am* coming home with you."

She nodded. "I know. And I want you to. It's just—"

"If this is about the Donahues giving you a hard time—" Had she thought he went too easy on Cody?

No, he couldn't believe that. Zoey was the most compassionate person he knew. She was also a woman wrongly targeted. "You know I'm on your side, right?"

"Oh, Garrett." She hugged him tight. "I loved how you dealt with Cody. That's actually one of the decisions I made."

"I don't understand."

Pushing back from him, she seemed to screw up her courage, then spoke in a rush of words that ran together. "I'm sorry because I know the timing is off and my mother is waiting and you have duties, but I haven't seen you since I made up my mind to do this, and if I don't do it now I might chicken out, so..."

"Hold up." This sounded serious, so maybe a little privacy was in order. Taking her arm, he steered her over to a park bench, out of the glaring sunshine. He ignored onlookers. He especially ignored Noel trying to get his attention. "Now." He wasn't entirely sure he wanted to know, but he asked anyway. "What's going on?"

She sucked in a very deep breath, then exhaled on a blurted, "I was wrong."

Uneasiness cut into him, tightening his jaw. "About?"

"Being friends with benefits."

Feeling lethal, and a little desperate, he reminded her, "You're the one who insisted on those benefits."

"I know!" She thrust out her hands. *"But I can't be just friends anymore."*

Getting a breath wasn't easy, so he just narrowed his eyes and waited.

"Garrett," she pleaded. "Don't look like that. I realize there's probably some right way to do this, but you know I was never any good at social etiquette."

"Screw etiquette." She didn't need to pretty it up for him. He wanted her to say it so he could get started convincing her otherwise. "Just spit it out."

"I'm messing this up so badly." She took his hand. "I *do* want you for a friend, yes."

Damn it. No way could he do that, not after being so much more.

"And sex, *yes*."

Okay, wait.

"But..."

With his heart suddenly thundering, Garrett nudged her. "But?"

She winced. "Am I being too bold?"

"No." *Be bold, Zoey.*

Behind them, Noel called out, "A little help here?"

He glanced back. Damn. Did everyone in Buckhorn want buttered corn? Looked like. Luckily, Amber strolled up to the booth just then. He saw Noel gesturing toward him, and he knew his sister would pitch in. When she sent him a thumbs-up, letting him know she had it covered, he nodded his gratitude.

Turning back to Zoey, he said, "Go on."

Uncertainty darkened her eyes.

"Hey." He smoothed her lips with his. "Remember, honey, you can tell me anything." And one way or another, he'd work it out with her.

"Right." Like a soldier, she came to attention and said quickly, "I care for you way beyond just being friends."

Now that was more like it. Satisfaction brought him closer, but he needed to hear her say it. "Tell me how much."

Her lips trembled. So did her small smile. She started to speak, but something beyond his shoulder caught her attention. She glanced there, then tipped her head for a longer look. "You know how I said I made two decisions?"

"Yeah."

She stood. "I'm sorry, but I need to take care of that second one right now."

No way. Halting her retreat, Garrett stood, too, followed her line of vision…and saw Carrie approaching. *Damn it, not now.*

Stiff and formal, Carrie stopped in front of him. She made a point of not looking at Zoey. "I knew you'd be here. I need to talk to you."

Sympathy weighed on him, but he had no idea what he could tell her.

Zoey knew. Smiling gently, she stepped around him to face Carrie. "I was hoping to see you here."

"I DON'T WANT to talk to you."

Though Carrie tried to turn away, Zoey saw the heartache in her eyes. "I know you're hurting." Talking over the music wasn't easy. The dancers had spilled from the stage to all around it.

Half urging, half pushing, she got Carrie to the bench they'd just vacated, then took her hand and didn't let go.

Scowling, Carrie strained away from her. "What are you doing?"

"I can't imagine losing a brother."

That stalled Carrie's animosity. "Gus is gone forever."

"I know." She'd been living with that fact for a very long time. "The thing is, Cody is still here."

"I know." She looked up at Garrett. "That's what I wanted to talk to you—"

"He's on the wrong path." Zoey regained her attention by saying, "And you know it."

She shook her head. "No, he just—"

"You might be the only family he has who knows it. He needs you, Carrie. He needs someone to care enough to not make excuses."

Carrie blanched. "I don't—"

"He needs you to start paying attention."

Taking that like a slap, Carrie said, "I'm not responsible for what he did!"

"Just as I wasn't responsible for what Gus did?"

When Carrie's bottom lip quivered, Zoey patted her hand.

"Believe me, I wish I had it to do over. I would have called the sheriff before Gus left. I would have called you. I would have…I don't know. Taken his keys."

At that, Carrie shared a tearful laugh with Zoey, because they both knew that hadn't been an option. For as long as she'd known him, Gus was a rage waiting to happen.

Taking the shared laugh as an opening, Zoey reached out for Carrie's other hand, too. "Unfortunately, we don't get do-overs. All we have is here and now, and your other brother, Cody, is here, *now*."

Carrie whispered, "I don't know what to do."

Looking over her shoulder at Garrett, Zoey said, "I bet you have a few ideas." She couldn't be wrong about that.

He looked surprised to be drawn in, but reassured her by agreeing. "I've been thinking about it."

Zoey beamed at him. "I knew you would."

"Yeah, you know me pretty well." He rested a hand on her shoulder. "I can't guarantee anything, but it's possible we could convince the sheriff to let Cody do some community time at the fire station. I wouldn't go easy on him. He needs to apologize to Zoey and rebuild the shed he burned. He needs to learn there are repercussions to the things he does."

"And," Zoey added, "he needs to understand the harm fire can do. It's not something he can play with."

Garrett nodded. "It won't be a picnic, but it'd be better than time in juvie."

Tears welled in Carrie's eyes. "You'd do that for him?"

So pleased that she almost couldn't contain herself, Zoey said, "Of course he would."

Garrett drew Zoey closer. "You'd have to convince your parents, and Carrie, we both know that's not going to be easy."

More resolute now, Carrie said, "Somehow I'll take care of it." She swallowed hard and admitted, "They mostly don't want to be bothered."

"He has you," Zoey told her. "Right?"

"Yes." Two shuddering breaths later, she managed a small smile and said to Zoey, "I don't understand you."

"You don't need to, as long as you understand Cody."

This time it was Carrie who squeezed Zoey's hands. "Thank you."

Content with how that had gone, Zoey watched her walk away.

Until Garrett tipped up her chin. "You were saying something about decisions?"

Wow, he'd jumped right back to that. "Yeah, um, decisions."

"I get that you decided to help Cody."

"Yes. That was one of my decisions. He's still young and his family is not easy—"

"And you know something about that, don't you?"

She did. "I knew you'd understand."

His smile seemed to touch her heart. "What else, honey?"

"I decided about you, too." If she didn't hurry it up he'd miss the entire fund-raiser because of her. "I don't mean to rush you, but I've decided that I want more."

He kissed her bottom lip, touched his tongue to her. "More with you? I like that idea."

Her heart stammered then stalled. "Not just sex." Then she amended, "Not that sex with you is ever *just* sex. That's not what I mea—"

"I love you, Zoey."

Her jaw dropped, but she recovered quickly. "That's what I was trying to say to you!"

Sinking his hands into her hair, he kissed her more urgently.

"You two are causing a scene."

They broke apart to see Shohn grinning down at them.

Garrett said, "Go help Amber and Noel with the damn corn."

"Right." He winked at Zoey, clapped Garrett on the shoulder and headed toward the booth.

Glad for the reprieve, Zoey rushed to say, "I'm not trying to pressure you. You have a house and I have a house and my mom is moving in and... Everything doesn't have to change right away. We could ease into things. Keep doing what we've been doing, because that's really working for me."

"Me, too."

"We could keep taking it one day at a time…"

Garrett hauled her close and kissed her quiet. "One day at a time works for me—as long as here on out, each day is with you." Then he said it again. "Because I love you."

She squeezed him tight. "I am so glad I came back to Buckhorn."

"It's where you belong," Garrett whispered. "Here—with me."

AMBER WAS SO busy watching her brother, she kept bumping into Noel. Not a terrible thing at all.

When Shohn came around the booth and started tying on an apron, she said, "I love it when a plan comes together."

Shohn gave her a look. "Been scheming again, huh?"

Smug, she said, "Think maybe we could make it a double wedding?"

He glanced at Noel. "You getting married?"

Noel choked.

Amber felt her face go hot, but she ignored it. "I meant you and Nadine, Garrett and Zoey."

"Hey, I'm game. Nadine and I are ready to set the date anyway. But you'll have to corral the others."

"I can handle that." She smiled…until she saw Noel shaking his head at her.

So he thought she was a busybody? So what. She gave him a look of disdain and asked, "Want to dance?"

Shohn's brows went up.

Noel just smiled as he handed his tongs to Shohn. "Thought you'd never ask."

* * * * *

ABOUT THE AUTHOR

Lori Foster is a *New York Times*, *USA TODAY* and *Publishers Weekly* bestselling author with books from a variety of publishers, including Berkley/Jove, Kensington, St. Martin's, Harlequin and Silhouette. Lori has been a recipient of the prestigious *RT Book Reviews* Career Achievement Award for Series Romantic Fantasy, and for Contemporary Romance. For more about Lori, visit her website at www.lorifoster.com.

Don't miss the other books in the Buckhorn Brothers series, available now from Lori and Harlequin HQN:

"*Buckhorn Ever After*" (in the Animal Attraction ebook anthology)

The Buckhorn Legacy

Forever Buckhorn

Buckhorn Beginnings